Get Off My L@wn

How a Computer Geek and His Wife Survived the Zombie Apocalypse

Perry S. Kivolowitz

I dedicate this work to my son Evan who pressed me to reengage in the zombie genre and to my wife Sara for being all a spouse should be and more.

And to George A. Romero.

◆ I am sorry for the people you lost.

The counselors say we "have to go on living." I wonder what the counselors really think, when they are alone and there is a sound or a smell and the memories bite and claw and moan. Do they repeat their own platitudes? Do they tell themselves to look on the bright side? Are they comforted that things could have been worse?

As you begin reading this, as evidenced by the fact that you even *can* begin reading this, take a moment to reflect on that last self-evident cliché. Things really could have been worse.

There have already been many memoirs written by survivalists and preppers. Some of these folks were down right tickled at the opportunity to crush rotting skulls with mail order Zombie Spikes.

There have been books written by soldiers who marshaled intense focus, fortitude and training to harness powerful weaponry or the solitary brutality of their own fists. Certainly, without these folks, none of us would be here.

Finally, there have been books written by completely ordinary folks who found strength and resolve to overcome the most extraordinary circumstances. These people are the true heroes.

Our story does not encompass the full sweep of the global melt down. We stayed close to home. This is not a grand epic. This is our account of a *great* tragedy writ *small*.

My wife Ruth Ann and I were not actively planning for the apocalypse. We gradually eased into it. Ruth Ann is a product of no-nonsense Midwestern farm stock. She has never taken shit from anyone. She brought a natural tendency towards preparedness and self-reliance common to small town America. I grew up in a rust belt city and was robbed, mugged and burgled so many times that I was finished being a victim. I brought a natural tendency towards worry and worshipped regularly at the altar of what-if.

Perhaps most importantly, I did not really like people much to begin with.

◆ Before we could build our "dream house", we had to do battle with a bunch of self-important pricks from the neighborhood association called the Architectural Review Committee. We picked our development because it was the most rural we could get while being new enough to get optical fiber to the house. The country that invented the Internet was finally catching up to Estonia (though we still lag far behind South Korea).

This part of Wisconsin is host to frequent tornadoes.

I did not want to be the guy interviewed on TV, head in hands, talking about how everything that was important to him was "gone, all gone." I wanted to be the guy next door to the guy whose house was gone, all gone. I wanted to be the guy whose house was 'miraculously untouched" by the fury of nature.

I do not believe in miracles but I do believe in Intelligent Design, as in, use some intelligence when you design a house in downtown tornadoville.

The pricks on the ARC wanted desperately to reject our house design and did so several times, much to the pleasure of our architect. The ARC whined that the house would look too much like a bunker. Each rejection served only to drive up our architect's fees and piss me off. Finally, we studied the neighborhood covenants closely and laid down the law to the architect. The committee approved our house design because we left them no way to reject it. We got our "bunker" by adding extra perennials, bushes, and some "mature" trees. We had to add a crap load of aluminum siding we did not need or want. On the ground floor, what were solid concrete walls were dotted with real shutters where windows would normally be.

Folks from the neighborhood flapped their jaws at how deep the foundation was being dug, "that's a mighty big hole you got there Doug." They scoffed at the tie rod reinforcement of the framing and they stopped talking to us altogether when they realized the tie rod reinforced framing was not that at all. It was reinforcement for poured concrete exterior walls. No, our neighbors did not like our house. Too damn bad for them I thought.

It really did turn out to be too damn bad for them because now they are "gone all gone." All except for us and the neighbor kid Ryan, who joined us for a while early on. He liked our house just fine.

◆ I made a hat full of money in Silicon Valley but no, you never heard of me. I was perfectly happy to let some Nehru shirt wearing wiener or snot nosed child dressed in black hog the camera. I was not the "god-like founder" type. I was a hit man brought in by venture capitalists when they needed somebody "to fully realize" the wiener's "vision." Four progressively bigger paydays and I kissed the Valley goodbye not needing to work again.

Being well off and having an eclectic set of interests helped Ruth Ann and me survive the near end of humanity. Our mix of mild paranoia and a well-developed cynicism definitely helped. To be honest, my worldview was simply "People suck." This turned out to be especially helpful when, in addition to sucking, people started biting, clawing and tearing too.

Were it only me in this mess I would have been out staggering on a long-term nature walk soon after the world went to shit. If it is not computer related, I am only as handy as a telephone and a credit card. I am Eva Gabor on Green Acres to Ruth Ann's Eddie Albert. She made our Fortress of Solitude possible.

◆ October dawned brisk and beautiful. The foliage had peaked early this year promising a cold winter. The local news bubbled with stories of folks looking forward to the start of bow and gun-hunting season in November, as was Ruth Ann. At the national level, it was the same shit different year. Those with more power fucked those with less. Those with none thought things were great never realizing how well and truly screwed they were.

Down in Madison the University was taking heat again for their research on H7N9, the 1918 flu, Ebola and other virus lines they never revealed they had. The Ebola research was supposed to have stopped back in 2009 but who knows if it was. In the years since, researchers at UW were in the news for publishing papers on how to tweak flu bugs to be more contagious and deadly. They claimed that knowing what few mutations were necessary to "enhance" the massively dangerous viruses would better prepare us should such mutation happen in the wild. "Forewarned is forearmed" they argued.

In reality, the University had spent millions building a first rate lab for some hotshot researcher they lured from some other place. They were not about to close down their investment "just because" the work might result in the end of the world.

Luckily, the flu bugs did not cause the end of the world.

The combination of flu bugs and aggressive viral meningitis (which they had not let on that they had) did.

In combining, much of the communicability of the flu was lost. The virus could live for only a short time airborne and on surfaces. Infection by proximity was a real potential. Transfer of bodily fluids had a guaranteed outcome.

The researchers were good at their jobs. They made a killer bug. Who said we couldn't build anything in America anymore? The lab facilities the UW built were as good as they said. They claimed the facilities were idiot proof. Maybe they were.

They were not, however, "$15.10 per hour Project-Assistant with one month on the job" proof.

The virus brought death after a mostly asymptomatic incubation period long enough for those infected to disperse. In a process, still not explained, reanimation occurred soon thereafter.

◆ Of all places, the first glimpse of what was to come broke on TMZ. Some celebutantes were in Madison for an annual charity benefit. There was an after-party at one of University Avenue's rowdier student bars. Madison and Wisconsin in general was great for bars. More bars than churches here, and we have a great many churches.

Come bar time the street was empty with the exception of folks with camera phones waiting for the celebs to exit. A kid (the lab assistant) came staggering down the street, a common sight that raised no eyebrows. He all but fell on one of the onlookers from behind and was filmed taking bites out of her.

People scattered but not without keeping their phones pointed at the bloody scene. After all, they were sure this would "go viral" and had visions of sugarplum fairies and zillions of virtual dollars dancing before their eyes. They were right about it going viral of course but I doubt anyone would be around to cash let alone issue the virtual checks.

The MPD was quickly on the scene. The "drunk" ignored police orders and warnings, tearing into the girl with teeth and nails. Finally distracted from his twitching victim by the shouting police officers, he made a move towards them. One cop fired his Taser. The drunk convulsed while the Taser's charge lasted but instead of remaining inert, got back up immediately. The cop fired the Taser's second load. Again, the drunk got back up as if nothing had happened.

Staggering at a patrolman with blood smeared arms outstretched and blood running down his chin onto his Sconnie sweatshirt, the cops put one shot each into the drunk's center of mass. The drunk went down and was still. One officer crouched low to feel for a pulse and reported he felt none. While still crouched, the drunk opened his eyes; he grabbed the cop's hand and yanked it quickly to his bloody mouth. The cop screamed from the pain of the vicious bite. The other cop fired into the drunk's head.

That was the footage that showed up on TMZ. After snarky comments about the cannibal missing out on a splitting headache in the morning, the segment closed with an exclamation of heartfelt thanks that the bimbo famous for being famous was safe. Thank heavens.

The widespread availability of several videos of the event immediately brought breathless online comments that the "dude's a zombie, bro." Unlike any fictional account of the zombie apocalypse that I have ever read, video of the first biting victim was globally available within twenty-four hours of the event. It did not make any difference.

◆ By that Friday (Day 3), there were reports around Dane County of similar bizarre behavior. The lab assistant had already spread the virus by aerosol to other students and academics. Those exposed to the police officers involved in the first recorded biting incident also spread the bug before they too expired and reanimated to bring mayhem by tooth and nail.

A community Fish Fry at a Cross Plains church became a scene of bewildered terror when a person in bloody and torn clothing entered the parish hall and began viciously biting parishioners. Similar events took place at a Fall Concert at a middle school in Waunakee, a high school varsity football game in Sun Prairie and an indie movie theater in Madison.

By the following Monday (Day 5), all schools (including the UW where this all began) in Dane and surrounding counties were closed. Reporters from all the major and not-so-major news organizations were flooding into Madison to report on events first hand. There were Internet-based reports of similar odd events taking place in a number of cities around the country and world.

The next day, Tuesday (Day 6) the Governor banned all forms of public assembly in southern Wisconsin. In protest, fourteen Wisconsin state legislators made public denouncements from an undisclosed location believed to have been in Illinois. We now know that one of these legislators was the local source of infection near the Wisconsin / Illinois border.

The Governor called out the National Guard in Dane County, declaring it a disaster area. By nightfall broadcasts from downtown Madison, right outside the ritzy hotel where the press was staying, showed the National Guard firing into a crowd of advancing bloody disfigured people. After warnings not to let small children watch what was about to come, bullets could be seen in slow motion entering and exiting persons who did not even falter. The segment closed with Guardsmen in violent hand-to-hand combat as strange attackers overran their positions.

On Wednesday (Day 7), the international news reported major uncontrolled outbreaks throughout the world.

◆ Back when the zombie apocalypse was fodder for fiction, most writers painted a bleak and hopeless future for humankind. Given the bug that actually hit us could spread indirectly by aerosol and contact (not just fluid transfer) bleak and hopeless looked about right.

Fortunately, we got the classic "slow dumb" zombie and not the lightning fast mutant ninja assassin zombies some fiction described. Who ever said they were "slow" must never been chased by one, ten or a thousand. They are not that slow.

What gave us hope from early on is that our zombies eventually rot. Given enough time and the right environmental conditions, their brainstems will eventually decay and detach. Waiting for that to happen though can kill you. Our government based its strategy upon patience. In the end, we would take back our country by concentrating on preserving life. There would be no nuclear or chemical weapons on U.S. soil.

On a global level, hot wet already stinky places like jungles were actually better off. The dead expired without help after less than eight weeks of mayhem. Cold places, like here in Wisconsin, have the mixed blessing of winter. The cold decreases their attention span. If you can hide, the chance they will wander off increases as the temperature drops. However, this benefit does not come without a significant downside. The cold extends the creature's shelf life indefinitely. In a deep freeze, they do not spoil at all.

Ironically, what were before the "best" places to live offering moderate weather all year became the very picture of bleakness described in the darkest of the pre-war books. On a personal note, I observe that my ex-wife still lived near Silicon Valley when it was wiped out. She was already a life-sucking bitch so things did not change that much for her.

On a local scale, on the scale of "up close and personal," on the scale of "we're surrounded by miles of pus," the theoretical advantages offered by any particular locale did not amount to much. Pundits used to say, "All politics is local." I do not need to tell you, "All zombies are local." One ambulatory zombie at your back is one more than you need.

The plague spread around the globe within a few weeks. Other writers can document in more detail how the international dominoes fell. Our story is primarily about our own patch of ground.

Was the course of events predictable? Absolutely.

If you have an Internet connection again, you can download the 2009 paper by Munz, Hudea, Imad and Smith from:

http://mysite.science.uottawa.ca/rsmith43/Zombies.pdf

Using basic modeling techniques, they came to the following conclusion:

> *"An outbreak of zombies infecting humans is likely to be disastrous, unless extremely aggressive tactics are employed against the undead. While aggressive quarantine may eradicate the infection, this is unlikely to happen in practice. A cure would only result in some humans surviving the outbreak, although they will still coexist with zombies. Only sufficiently frequent attacks, with increasing force, will result in eradication, assuming the available resources can be mustered in time."*

Initial reaction in the U.S. was laughable. In those first few days we tweeted, "liked," LOL'd and OMG'd the approaching end-of-days. There was a seemingly non-stop stream of pictures with witty captions. Americans grasped the full impact of what was happening later Wednesday morning. The shocking video of dying National Guardsmen from the night before had now been seen by every American with access to any media device.

Later in the day, the city that birthed the plague became the first city in the world declared an uninhabitable military zone.

Losing a state capital, home to more than 250,000, stopped the idiotic meme machine cold.

The news did not stop a different type of idiot: ideologically driven lawyers.

The Federal Government attempted large-scale mobilization on Friday (Day 9) but lawsuits seeking to stop or limit action brought those efforts to a standstill. The far left wanted "to study the impact on the rights of those affected." The far right, who were convinced the liberal leaning President finally had his pretext to take their guns away, insisted the U.S. military could not be allowed to act within the United States under Posse Comitatus laws. Fortunately, the well-regulated militia actually envisioned by the framers, the National Guard, was not similarly impeded.

◆ Ruth Ann and I discussed what our course of action would be, as things got worse. From the start we figured we were better off right here at home than facing the unknown of relocation. The neighborhood Architectural Review Committee had whined that our house would look like a bunker. We compromised by adding more curb appeal, but they were right. We *had* built a bunker.

We completed our contingency inventories. We were already well supplied. Just the same, I charged my Amazon credit card up to its credit limit on whatever survival supplies we felt we needed. With any luck, the items would be here by Tuesday. Ruth Ann told me which bow supplies, red dot, IR and laser optics to order for each weapon we owned. I bought boatloads of uncommon battery types to complement the many dozens of standard rechargeables we had, survival gear like food and hand tools, firearm-training equipment (I did not have a clue) and many Kindle-based reference books. I figured if UPS made it, great. If not, I would argue for a refund if we lived or Visa would have a tough time collecting if we did not.

After lunch, we rounded up all the cash we had on hand. Ruth Ann put her carbine in the car with spare ammo. There were two mom-and-pop arms dealers within four miles of our house. Ah, Wisconsin! We figured that the bigger dealers would run out of inventory first. Our intent was to stock up on anything she found to augment our own supplies. We agreed someone should remain at the house. That someone would be me as my weapons knowledge extended no further than the Military Channel before it went all reality TV.

As we opened the garage, we could see nothing much out of the ordinary except for more kids than one would expect at this time on a weekday. Our neighborhood had many young families so with schools closed now across the state there were kids out playing. One thing that was odd was every child had an active and watchful set of adult eyes on them. No child was unsupervised. Neighbors talked together in driveways or backyards with eyes locked on their kids.

"Hey Ruth Ann," a woman Ruth Ann knew waved her down.

"Hi Amanda, how are you?"

"Pissed off! I went to my yoga class this morning and the damn place was closed. So I went for a latte at Starbucks and it was closed too. I waited around a whole hour for my nail appointment and they closed up shop while I was sitting there! I am not having a good day!"

"I'm sure it will get better Amanda, just give it a chance."

"It better. Emma's school being closed is really cramping my day. What am I supposed to do with my time, clean and cook?" Amanda burst out laughing.

Ruth Ann feigned a giggle and made her good byes.

On turning west onto US 12 Ruth Ann noticed a little more traffic than usual made up of loaded family cars with suitcases and such on roof racks. These stood out because we lived far off the path beaten by FIPs ("Friendly" Illinois People) to their vacation homes. Folks from the Twin Cities did not vacation much around here either. She stopped at the BP, topped off the Volvo, and filled a pair of small gas cans. She said there were a couple of cars waiting ahead of her for one of the four pumps. Having to wait at all was a bit unusual.

There were a number of cars parked along 12 and the side street at the gun shop. If they were having a sale, that wouldn't be unusual but they didn't have sales even before the zombie apocalypse. The little shop was quite crowded. Prices had gone up a lot too.

"Hey Freddie. The place is hopping," Ruth Ann said to the owner. "I haven't seen this many people in here since never."

"Yeah, been like this since Tuesday when the Governor brought out the Guard in Dane County. There is nothing like a crisis to pay for fixing my kid's teeth. Orthodontia, there's a criminal enterprise."

"What's with the prices Freddie, you're practically a war profiteer."

"Supply and demand Ruth Ann. I didn't invent it. What do you need?"

"Need? I hope I don't need anything. But what I want is more ammo. What do you have left in .308 and .30? I want to have some punch when I reach out and touch something."

"I can let you have four boxes of .308 hollow points, they make a big impression, and six boxes of .30 unless you want to take a spam can off my hands."

Ruth Ann looked at the price on the huge box of .30 carbine rounds known as a "spam can" and whistled.

"I can't afford that Freddy. I will take the others. Can't hook me up with more?"

"Ruth Ann, after I sell these to you I'm going to raise the price another 20 percent. I'm just about out of these."

"I appreciate the deal Freddie. Can you spare some 38 Specials too? We can use it if things look grim."

"Yeah, I can sell you four boxes. How are you fixed for shotgun shells, I have a lot of 20 and 28 gauge left. Seems folks want more punch."

"I don't have any shotguns."

Freddie's head notched back a tad in surprise. He thought she was a native Badger. He changed the subject.

"So you going to stay in that bunker of yours?"

At this, a smelly man in hunter's blaze orange covers perked up, looking directly at Ruth Ann.

"Oh, Freddie, you know it's not a bunker. I'm hurt that you think so," Ruth Ann said coyly.

She settled up and was on her way out when she noticed the guy in orange talking with Freddie and pointing rather obviously at her.

Ruth Ann came away with about half the ammo she thought our money would buy. On the way back, Ruth Ann stopped at the BP again and was surprisingly able to withdraw a modest amount from the ATM. She figured we might need the cash later on, past when ATM machines ceased to function. When she left, she thought she saw a guy in a pickup pull out onto 12. He was wearing orange.

That night we started keeping our police scanner on. I used to tell people that every family should have a scanner if only to get a sense of how hard working and courageous their local law enforcement was. Some disembodied voice tells a policewoman to investigate a report of shots fired in the middle of a moonless night alone and her only answer might be, "Four minutes out." People just had no appreciation for how good they had it.

This night's radio calls mostly centered upon rotating vehicles into maintenance garages to pick up extra supplies and equipment. There were also more than the usual amount of assisting distressed motorists, traffic violations and accidents. It sounded more like a summer Saturday night than an October Friday.

The news had finally gone O.J. over the virus. It was now "all virus, all the time." CNN reduced their commercials and put on Wolf Blitzer to repeat the same stories over and over again hour after hour. Wolf Blitzer is like the Jerry Lewis MDA telethon of bad news. If Wolf is on screen for more than an hour, something is terribly wrong in the world.

Metropolitan areas across the U.S. were showing the beginning signs of a terminal spiral into chaos. The Feds were still operating with an arm tied behind their backs. Use of the regular service branches was still held up in court. Across the globe, however, U.S. assets were heading home. Now we know what it takes to bring all the troops home.

Bases across the country were running on a war footing and were feverishly, sorry - bad choice of words - hurriedly laying in supplies and bulking up defenses.

Components of the Military Sealift Command and Ready Reserve Fleet that weren't already underway or prepositioned were being loaded out around the clock. Ships that were prepositioned overseas were steaming homeward. Efforts were underway to make ready lesser-used merchant marine assets.

In retrospect, it is obvious that those in charge of logistics and force disposition were showing a vote of no confidence in a strategy focused on containing the infected. If outbreaks were expected to be contained, it would mean that overland transport, perhaps agriculture and some manufacturing might continue. Putting massive quantities of supplies out to sea showed planners were preparing for the necessity to resupply through extraordinary means, not through the usual channels. Clearly, some parts of the Federal government were on top of their game.

◆ On this day, Saturday (Day 10), we had a list of things to do around the house. Our goal of remaining at home seemed realistic because of its bunker-like construction. The exterior walls were made entirely of poured reinforced concrete. Our living areas were on the second floor. Our first floor had guest bedrooms, an office, laundry, main entry and a den. All of the windows visible on the exterior of the first floor were facades; window shutters covering concrete. Instead, natural lighting on the first floor came from narrow horizontal strip windows high up.

Tough as our shell might have been, we figured our survival also depended on stealth. Before we could enforce "light discipline", we needed to implement it. First, we spray painted all first floor glass black. When that paint ran out, we switched to the kind used for weather proofing outdoor furniture. We wadded much of our bed linens into the strip windows to backstop the paint.

On the second floor, we began by closing the shutters to match the fakes below. We saved our heavier fabrics for use upstairs especially over the sliding glass door at the deck. These were stapled in place with the exception of using Velcro at the deck door.

◆ We were friendly only with two neighbors. The Boetche's were across the street to the north of us and their neighbor to the northeast, the Flynn's. Denny Boetche was a day trader leveraging the super high speed of the neighborhood's fiber based Internet. Meg Boetche was a stay-at-home mom though their son Ryan was off at school at UW Green Bay. They were transplants from New York.

Robert and Nancy Flynn were native Wisconsinites. Bob owned a company specializing in asbestos abatement and replacing older office building lighting systems with energy efficient lighting. To be honest, I don't know what Nancy did with her days but Ruth Ann did. I knew Bob was a hunter. We'd been in his house for cocktails and saw a few mounted trophies.

He and Ruth Ann talked hunting talk while I talked to Nancy about the weather, the Packers and computer malware. They had lots. I wish I had worn my black tee shirt from ThinkGeek that said "No I won't fix your computer." But, I didn't, so I did.

This afternoon Denny Boetche was in his backyard. He saw me while I was walking the grounds with a 10 inch tablet checking the field of view on our security cameras. He came over to talk.

"Hey Doug. Looks like you and Ruth Ann are going to make a stand," he said.

"We think we'll be better off here than who knows where. What are your plans?"

"We'll be leaving soon. The news is so incredible. It has to burn itself out. Meg and I will sit tight at our cottage in Door County. It'll be over before we get the cottage cleaned up."

"You think so? You haven't seen enough zombie movies."

"There you go again, always thinking the worst is going to happen."

"It usually does. What was that truck delivering last week?"

"Oh, for Meg's herbs. We put in a generator to keep the sun lamps on in the basement. She's got prize oregano and basil coming in. We don't want to lose it."

"I didn't know you guys were so serious about gardening."

"Yeah Ruth Ann's been a huge help. What do you think she and Meg talk about during their afternoon teas on your roof?"

"I figured they talked about me and you, mostly."

"That too. Listen, I had a hard time finding enough gas to fill the generator's tanks. Do you have any to spare?"

"I could loan you a five gallon can," I hated to let go of one of the cans Ruth Ann just filled up but Denny saw us unload them. I couldn't say no.

"Thanks. That'll add about 10 hours to the weeks' worth we have now."

"You think all you'll need is a week? Come on Denny, it's almost been a week since we lost a whole city for shit's sake. Things are getting worse, not better."

"Well, whatever. Come over tomorrow morning before we go, OK? I have something for you to remember us by."

"Sure. About nine OK?"

"Make it eight. See you."

◆ Turns out Denny and Meg were timely in deciding to leave. On the radio Sunday morning (Day 11), the state emergency preparedness agency started advising all persons to join up with National Guard units escorting folks to "safe zones" that were being set up. For our area, Chippewa Valley Regional Airport was being turned into a refugee center.

It was a good choice for a safe zone. The airport had plenty of open space, not too many homes nearby and was protected on three sides by the Chippewa River. At only ten miles away, Denny and Meg might even be able to come back to take care of their herbs from time to time. However, they were set on heading to their cottage instead. I could not blame them, as it was a beautiful place far from population centers.

Denny and Meg were all packed up in their SUV when I went over there at eight. A Humvee had already come through the neighborhood announcing that there would be a rally point on U.S. 12 a little bit east of here for an eight thirty departure over to the airport. The destination was so close and familiar one had to wonder why an escort might be needed.

Denny handed me a tall potted plant wrapped for protection in a black plastic garbage bag.

"Thanks, Denny. I'll bring this up to the greenhouse," I said.

"It'll do great up there in all that sunshine. We've always envied that greenhouse you've got hidden up there."

"Are you heading to the airport safe zone?"

"No, our plans are still Door County. We're going to head out now before we get stuck behind the group heading to the airport."

We shook hands. "Well, send us a postcard."

"Will do Doug. Take care. Say goodbye to Ruth Ann for us."

Denny and Meg Boetche drove away in their packed up SUV. We never saw them again. Months later, their SUV was found in the parking lot of a Comfort Inn off WI 29 near Shawano. The roads near there were unnavigable later on but when Denny and Meg left, there should have been smooth sailing. We will never know why they stopped there or what happened to them.

I brought the plant back to our house and handed it off to Ruth Ann. She brought it into the kitchen to unwrap it. While checking my email I called out to Ruth Ann “Is it the oregano or the basil?”

“What?”

“Is the plant oregano or basil? Denny said they had a prize winning crop coming in.”

“It’s a prize winner alright but I don’t think it’s oregano *or* basil. Come here and take a look for yourself.”

I poked my head into the kitchen to see Ruth Ann watering what she told me was a fine example of Mendocino Mind Fuck. I wondered how she knew what variety the plant was. The Berkeley of the Midwest might belong to the undead but the Mendocino of the Midwest would be alive and well, and living on my roof.

◆ The remainder of the day was surreal.

A new word had been seared into the public's consciousness, "horde." The undead were not solitary creatures. They seemed to be attracted by whatever attracts one of their colleagues. Like a snowball rolling downhill they collect more of themselves into bigger and bigger groups. As they increase in numbers, they become unstoppable. They simply overwhelm any defense put in their path. In China, hordes were said to number in the hundreds of thousands and were still growing.

They were like a plague of locusts leaving nothing alive as they move through. There was an aerial shot of a horde moving through the dormitories and factories in Shenzhen. Repetitive metaphors be damned, they were like a horde of worker ants. Like a tsunami, the force of so many bodies compressed in small spaces burst windows and caved in storefronts. They oozed through tight spaces widening gaps until torrents flowed through the broken and crushed obstacle. After a few minutes of watching, metaphors failed. A horde was not like anything else.

At two PM, the Governor declared martial law to be in effect within the borders of the State Of Wisconsin. As the virus originated at a research lab at the University of Wisconsin Madison, there has never been nor likely ever be a more compelling example of the Wisconsin Idea that says the fruits of the University should have an impact felt across the whole state.

The Governor advised all citizens to proceed to one of several safe zones in the state, a list of which scrolled continuously at the bottom of the screen. He told us that emergency information would be broadcast continuously on several AM frequencies. He blessed us, wished us luck and scurried off to wherever it is that the rich and powerful go when the dead go walking.

Throughout the rest of the day, we watched our neighbors leave one by one. It was irritating when an adult face stared at us as they drove past. The adult faces read, "You assholes think you're so smart, don't you." It was heartbreaking however, when the face peered out of the car window belonged to a child. The children's faces read fear, confusion and sadness.

◆ By Tuesday (Day 13), events finally overwhelmed the legal debate freeing the Federal government to act. And act decisively they did: to quarantine.

Quarantine was predicted to be the opposite of the right course of action by Munz et al. In actuality, it ensured a steady supply of prey to the predators, much like misguided zoning laws aimed at increasing diversity. Quarantine doomed urban survivors to virtually certain death, as hordes grew in size with every passing minute.

Troops manned makeshift fortified lines surrounding major population centers. It was a hopeless waste of time, resources and the precious treasure of human life. One look at the Shenzhen footage should have convinced everyone that short defensive lines keeping them out would be better than long thinly stretched lines trying to keep them in.

Almost two weeks after TMZ broadcast the first zombie attack and two days since the declaration of martial law in the state the most amazing and unexpected thing happened. A UPS truck pulled up to the house and delivered some of the items I had ordered on Friday! The driver had a real sense of humor. He laughed maniacally when he told us we were his last delivery. I was glad when he left. He was scary.

◆ Wednesday (Day 14), brought several more changes. I noticed the news items on the major sites were not being updated as frequently as they had been. CNN's web site was the most sporadic.

Their broadcast news showed the Atlanta streets around CNN Center teeming with moving corpses. Wolf Blitzer was not on the air any longer. Instead, someone much younger I had never seen before was on standing in what looked like a stairwell.

"The dead have crashed through all the glass at street level. The elevators have been disabled for our security and the lower level stairwells have been blocked with whatever people can find."

The camera tilted downward. While there wasn't anything but the next landing to see there was a terrific pounding booming up from below.

"The sounds you are hearing are the dead. They are beating against the elevator and stairwell doors. They don't stop. No one here expects the doors to last indefinitely. We have CNN security and Atlanta PD here with us but we just showed you the crush outside. If they beat down the doors there isn't anything we'll be able to do to stop them."

The camera was back on the newcomer. Camera and reporter moved out of the stairwell into a floor of cubicles.

"And even if the doors hold, you can see we're not exactly equipped for a siege. When the emergency supplies are exhausted and the vending machine food is gone, we know we are going to starve. Water pressure here in CNN Center has been fluctuating. There's a chance we will run out of water before we run out of food."

The camera centered on the kid's face. Its youth was gone. His eyes were wet, tired, red and puffy. He had several days of stubble that would have been considered a risky career move before all this. He said nothing for a bit. Then he began shaking his head. The camera pulled back. The kid was looking away from the camera and waving his hand to shut down.

"Bob, that's it. I can't do this anymore. Go find Deborah. I can't do this" An infographic replaced the kid.

I had to think that an organization like CNN would keep things together better than the kid was making it out to be. There must be a helipad on their building, right? There is no way an organization like that would let their people die, trapped in their own headquarters. But that is what happened.

I do not know what became of the kid. I haven't seen him since broadcasts resumed. His report was the last broadcast television Ruth Ann and I saw for a very long time.

The power grid failed later that evening. I took a camp light to the mechanical room and made the necessary changes at the breaker panel and electrical box. We would be running key services off the solar charged batteries in the basement from here on out. At the breaker panel, I made sure breakers for lines we weren't going to use were switched off to prevent mistakes. The loss of local power took down our Internet access as well. The world as Ruth Ann and I appreciated it was shutting down.

The other big change was the police scanner. Teams of deputies were pairing with National Guard troops to engage the dead as they were found near the safe zone at the airport. Their strategy was sound. Engage the dead only from intersections to maximize escape options. They picked off ghouls from outside their patrol vehicles. If the dead got close, they'd get back into their car and move to another intersection. The dispatch center helped the teams to keep to intersections where they could render mutual aid.

We heard no one lose his or her life on this day.

Ruth Ann wondered aloud "If all the deputies are in Chippewa Falls, who is patrolling out here?"

She knew the answer.

◆ The answer was confirmed the next morning, Thursday (Day 15). Dispatchers on the scanner told any officers listening that looting was taking place across the area. They were ordered *not* to intercede if they saw any. In fact, law enforcement was ordered to stop enforcing *any* laws. All personnel were needed at the safe zone.

Ruth Ann and I were up on the roof. She was tending the garden, getting some fresh greens together for lunch. I was keeping watch. That is to say, I was keeping her company and was aimlessly looking at the scenery. I heard a crash from the road to our east. Across the open yards and tall grasses, a large blue pickup truck sat in the driveway two houses north, the Xian's house. I quietly called Ruth Ann over and we watched from the cover of the parapet wall. The bed of the pickup was partially filled with stuff. The stuff looked tossed together, not like someone packing their own possessions in an organized way.

A front window had been bashed in to make entry into the home. The front door was open now. A large man with a rifle stepped out the front door, looked around then looked back at the door. He made a "come on" motion with his hand. Two other men with rifles slung on their backs came out of the door carrying boxes. We could not see what they had; just that it was boxes piled with more differently colored stuff.

Looters had come to the neighborhood.

We watched them make a few more trips back into the house. Two of the men walked to the next house in our direction belonging to the James'. The big man got in the truck and drove it to the next driveway. Getting out of the truck with a baseball bat, he walked up to the front door and bashed in the sidelight near the door lock. As he strode back to the truck to toss the bat in the cab, a partner reached in through the broken glass and undid the door's lock. The big guy resumed his watch and the other two went to work clearing out what they wanted.

"We better get ready for them," I said to my wife.

She went for her hunting rifle and the carbine with a supply of ammunition for both. I went to the garage and brought up an old portable P.A. system I had from my days doing trade shows. At 150 watts it would be ear splitting in what was otherwise silence. I would speak loudly and Ruth Ann would carry a high powered stick.

While I was setting up and trying to remember how the P.A. worked, Ruth Ann set up in a prone position with a view of our own road and driveway through a drainage port. We were set and had agreed on a plan by the time the men cleared out the last house, the Olson's, before ours. They all hopped in the truck to make the slightly longer trip to our road. I watched them approach our road with the security camera tablet app so that I remained completely hidden. I flipped on the P.A.

As they made the turn to enter our road I put on my best "boss" voice.

"Driver! Halt! Halt or be fired upon."

The truck lurched to a stop, heads turned inside the cab trying to pinpoint the source of the sound.

"You had your fun. Back up and leave."

We could see the movement inside the cab. Ruth Ann and I agreed we would push them fast and hard to keep them disoriented. We figured these were not professional looters but more "looters of opportunity." We wouldn't give them a chance to form a plan. Ruth Ann fired a round that exploded the driver's side headlight.

"Driver! That was your headlight. The next one will be your head. Leave now. No more warnings." That was the coolest thing I've ever said out loud.

The truck backed up and burned rubber away out of the neighborhood.

"We better keep a close watch tonight," Ruth Ann said.

"Think they'll come back, do you?"

"They're males. Males always want something more when somebody says they can't have it. We just told them they can't have this house. If they're like most men, they'll be back."

"Ah," time to change subject I thought. "We can't risk losing any of our cameras and I'd hate to lose a window," I said. The shutters upstairs were closed matching the inoperable shutters on the first floor. They were there to protect the second floor glass from windblown debris. I didn't expect them to fair well against bullets.

"The cameras are up high, they may not have even noticed them. The real windows are on the second floor so they're up high too. Sounds like we need to keep their attention on the first floor where they can't hurt anything."

Ruth Ann was right. The thugs had already demonstrated their preferred means of breaking in, a baseball bat to a ground floor window or door. I wasn't worried about our front door. Even if they did to us what they did to the James' house, it would do them no good. They could get to the door's deadbolt but they couldn't reach its twin hasps. It would be hilarious to watch them try and break into our first floor "windows." Good luck to them with that.

"Laser gun sights are intimidating, right?" I said.

"Yeah very, but they tell the bad guys exactly where you are."

"Perfect."

I told Ruth Ann what I had in mind for a diversion. She thought it was worth a try. Over the remainder of our lunch we talked strategy.

"If we're going to defend our castle Doug, you are going to have to shoot somebody. Lucky for us, too bad for them, it is a full moon tonight. I'll put a red dot scope on the carbine. All you have to do is put the red dot on your target and squeeze the trigger."

"But a laser will tell them where I am, you said."

"A laser is different from a red dot. A laser reaches out and touches the target. A red dot glows just inside your own scope. Nobody else can see it."

"Got it. But I've never shot anything before. Let alone a person."

"At this range all you have to do is line up the dot, relax and squeeze. If you're having an inner moral conflict it's the easiest one of all to work out. Either you kill them or they kill you. Any questions?"

I opened my mouth to say something. But I closed it again. There was nothing to say.

◆ I had a classroom's worth of Raspberry Pi's in the house that I was preparing to donate to the local middle school. The Pi is a credit card sized full blown computer that was designed in England by a charitable foundation seeking to teach kids about technology. They are easy to program and consume next to no power. One of the things they are great at is controlling other devices. For instance, a Pi can control relays on another little board to turn lamps on and off. For every Pi I had, I had an eight channel relay board to go with it.

Ruth Ann drilled a hole about the diameter of a pencil in four shutters on the sides of the house, two each to the northeast and southwest. I broke the laser diodes out of some laser pointers and presentation remote controls. I soldered up new leads to their power pins. They take 3 volts at less than a watt. Easy enough.

Ruth Ann just barely attached the laser diodes inside the shutters. We would let the wind cause a little movement so the beams didn't just sit there. I ran speaker wire up to the roof and connected each side's pair of diodes to a Pi connected to a relay board. I wrote a little Python program that caused the diodes to turn on for three seconds at a time at random intervals.

The net effect was that it would look like there were four shooters in the "windows" peering through the shutters. If the bad guys were going to shoot at something, their first and maybe last shots might be at solid concrete hidden by aluminum siding.

We tried to come up with a way of protecting the greenhouse and solar panels. Coming up with nothing, we hoped to engage them when they were close enough not to be able to see those vital but fragile structures at all from ground level.

◆ Today's radio update brought two pieces of international news. The Queen of England and Prince Philip had been killed. Like her father during World War II, Elizabeth chose to stay in London during her people's greatest need. The Royal Family was safe within a bunker far below the city's streets. Someone in her household staff smuggled in a family member who died and reanimated inside the Royal Apartments themselves. The whereabouts of her successors were not immediately known. The United Kingdom would know a state of interregnum not experienced since the 17th century.

The other news told that Canada had offered blanket admission to all Americans provided they not transit the border at established crossings. Crowding at the formal crossings resulted in massive carnage from uncontrolled infection. Canadians and fleeing Americans were urged to gather in small groups and use Canada's vast expanses of emptiness as their defense. The Canadian government moved to the large island in the Manicouagan Reservoir. One asteroid killed the dinosaurs. Another saved the Canadian command authority.

◆ At three AM on Friday morning, (Day 16), Ruth Ann saw the glow of headlights on McKenzie Road, an east west road that runs past our neighborhood. There is a berm parallel to McKenzie lined with trees shielding our development from the road but it was easy enough to see the glow come to a stop and then go out.

The berm and its neighboring open space are about twenty yards wide. Then, an east west road inside our development runs past our block. That's another ten yards. Finally, our corner house is set back on the south by about thirty yards. Once clearing the trees on the berm, these guys would have to cross more than forty yards of open ground with next to no cover lit up by a full moon. If we had to be visited by armed looters we could be thankful they were stupid armed looters.

A total of five men poked cautiously out of the trees. A pair appeared just to the west of us, they'd try the front of the house. A trio appeared just to the east. They'd try the back. Ruth Ann quietly shifted over to cover the trio, I drew the pair. Each man carried a rifle. One of mine was dressed in hunter's blaze orange. He did not blend into the background.

The others dressed in darker winter coats. They inched closer. I put the P.A. system away earlier which was good because I was so tempted to shout "We can see you, you know." But I didn't.

We waited until they reached our lawn. I hate people on my lawn. Not that I care about the lawn itself as a body of grass. For all I care it could be green painted asphalt. The thing is it's my fucking lawn and you don't come on it unless you're invited.

Like all "good" gunfights, in addition to surviving, this one was over quickly.

I triggered the phony laser gun sights. One of my guys dropped to the ground and one of Ruth Ann's did as well. All five rifles aimed at the first floor. I actually fired before Ruth Ann. I put the red dot on the center of standing guy's chest and didn't hesitate. The view through the red dot sight made it look a little like a video game. That's how I put out of my mind that I was squeezing the trigger of a real gun pointed at real person. I breathed in, let a little out then squeezed the trigger. I felt myself jerk in anticipation of the recoil.

I missed. But not by much, standing guy decided right then he'd had enough and turned around running.

Ruth Ann's hunting rifle had cycled twice while I moved in slow motion. Two of her targets who had fired at the first floor were dead with headshots. Only two targets remained between us.

Both lifted their rifles up to the second floor. My guy was prone - it was hard for him to angle upwards. As he did, I got to look him straight in the eye when I squeezed my trigger. One shooter left.

That one took a bite out of the wall a few inches from its top demonstrating he had no idea we were firing through the drainage ports at the floor of the roof. Ruth Ann made her hat trick.

And that was that.

◆ Ruth Ann and I awoke in the late morning of Friday (Day 16). We were still in our clothes sprawled out on the living room couches. We hadn't talked much about how we spent our night. We killed four people. Ruth Ann looked into me and knew what I was thinking.

"Nobody forced them to come back, Doug. That they were here at all is proof enough of their intent."

"I know."

"So none of this self-doubt and what ifs you obsess on, OK?"

Maybe she didn't know what I was thinking.

"That's not it hon. It's that, well, there are four dead guys on our lawn. What the fuck do we do with them?"

"Oh… That is a good question. You got yours in the head right? We won't be seeing them walking around again, that's good. We've got that going for us."

"How about dumping them in one of the houses they broke into?"

"We can't bury them. The ground is too hard for us to dig in. Yeah, that would be good karma I suppose. What goes around comes around."

"Let's get to it then. I'd rather throw up on an empty stomach and not waste any food."

First, we checked the security cameras. There was no activity outside except some crows picking at the looters' remains. We watched for a few minutes anyway, cycling through the cameras one by one so we could hear the output of their mikes. Just crow and wind noises.

We went to the garage. I tossed some garbage bags in the car and manually raised the door for Ruth Ann to back the car out. Ruth Ann moved the wagon over to the first body. *My* first body I should say. It was the moron in the orange hunter covers.

Ruth Ann looked at the cadaver and said, "I've seen this fucker before. He followed me out of Freddie's gun shop the other day. Freddie had said we lived in a bunker and this guy perked up."

"Well, he found us. Sucks for him."

Ruth Ann checked out his weapon and looked through his pockets for anything useful he might have carried. We didn't bother looking at his ID. Looter J. Looter was enough ID for us. I worked a garbage bag over the guy's head. Ruth Ann said his rifle matched her .308 hunting rifle caliber so we would be keeping it. Together we put the guy feet first most of the way into the bed of our wagon.

I walked on to the group of three that Ruth Ann had dispatched while she drove the car with its hatch still up. We were just starting our work when the sound of heavy engines scared the shit out of us.

Looking up, a line of four Humvees was heading right for us. Each had a soldier standing behind an M60 machine gun.

I'm stuffing a guy's head into a garbage bag and Ruth Ann has her hands in his pockets. There are two more dead guys next to us and one more hanging out the back of our car. I was hoping Ruth Ann would say "Let me do the talking." But she didn't.

◆ The lead Humvee stopped near us. I watched with dismay as two of the M60's turned in our direction. A tired looking lieutenant exited the Humvee's passenger side. One hand rested above his undrawn side arm. His other held a clipboard. I got even more nervous as clipboards can be more dangerous than guns.

"Mr. and Mrs. Handsman?" he said half looking at us half at his clipboard.

"Yes, that's us. How can we help you?" I said sounding like an idiot.

"I am Lieutenant Mancheski, Wisconsin National Guard. Who are your friends?"

"Looters. They did those three houses yesterday," I pointed, "and came for us at three this morning."

"I see," he looked at the looted homes then at the corpses. I could see in his face he was done thinking about three dead looters.

"Mr. Handsman, sir, this is our last time through the area. If you wish to come with us, we can escort you to the safe zone. The number of walkers we are running into is increasing quickly. We cannot protect you out here..." He nodded towards the bodies.

"Thanks for your offer Lieutenant. My wife and I are committed to riding things out here at home. We'll be fine."

"Mr. Handsman, sir, you do know what is coming right? You know what's been going on?"

"We do. Maybe "riding things out" makes it sound like we aren't being realistic. We know what is coming. We want to be in our own home when it gets here."

"OK. I understand. I need you to sign this sir, if you please." I could see in his face he was done thinking about two crazy homeowners too.

He handed me his clipboard. I removed my bloody gloves and took the clipboard to read over. It was a waiver of liability.

Both Ruth Ann and I signed the waiver that said we had refused the government's offer of "limited liability" sanctuary and if anything happened to us we couldn't sue for damages.

When I had handed the clipboard back to Lieutenant Mancheski he said, "Maybe you folks are making the right choice. There are too many people at the airport already. There is talk of hordes forming in the Twin Cities, Milwaukee and Illinois. How are we supposed to defend against them?"

He looked exhausted and sad.

"It'll be OK young man. Things will work out," Ruth Ann, the kindly woman who had just killed three guys, comforted the man sent to rescue us.

We parted shortly after. The Lieutenant offered "free haul away service" of our four unwanted guests. We did not volunteer the rifle we already stowed in the car and the Guardsmen politely didn't ask for it. Each of the Humvees left with a mason jar of Ruth Ann's homemade strawberry preserves.

◆ I want to revisit and expand why Ruth Ann and I had decided days ago that we would refuse every invitation to go for a ride. As I've described before, it isn't that we didn't trust the government. We didn't trust our fellow citizens.

Why would we leave? Surrounded by concrete we had more than 1200 square feet of solar electric panels on a flat parapet style roof. Shielded by the parapet wall, we could be on the roof hidden from anyone or anything on ground level.

The solar array fed battery storage in the basement. Used judiciously, power was not a problem.

We are on well and septic. The water pump only took 600 watts. We could top off the bathtubs, sinks and other containers each day without killing our power budget. We use stored water rather than the taps for routine usage.

Next to the solar panels, Ruth Ann kept a small greenhouse useable all year round. She grew various greens, onions and a barrel full of potatoes. These were hardy, resource efficient and mostly self-sustaining crops.

We stored up a large amount of homemade canned goods. We had all the survival food we recently purchased in addition to stores we had accumulated over the years. A prudent California family keeps some emergency food in case of earthquakes. A nervous California family keeps a lot of emergency food in case of earthquakes.

The garage, front, back and sliding doors were all commercial grade and set in steel frames. One too many break-ins experienced as a child convinced me of the value of investing in doors that would stand up to baseball bats. The first floor windows were fakes and the upstairs windows had shutters and were out of reach.

If something can be used as a weapon, Wisconsin had a dedicated hunting season just for it. We had three guns in the house, now four, with plenty of ammunition. Ruth Ann was her high school's varsity archery team captain. We even had Ruth

Ann's brother's black powder musket, (but with no black powder, it would be useful only as a club).

With eight day / night security cameras around the perimeter of the house, we had great 'situational awareness." The cameras were hooked up to an SSD-based DVR. The whole system consumed less power than a hundred watt light bulb. In fact, with regard to technology, we could be our own big box store. Add tablets, WIFI, phones (the WIFI on them worked even with cell service gone) to the Pi's, we had an enormous low power information processing capacity. I was not sure how all the IT would translate in this dead new world but at least we'd be able to keep up our skills launching birds at pigs.

We trusted each other, Ruth Ann and I, more than we trusted a few thousand strangers. Inside our house, we had the opportunity for self-determination. In a camp, we would be members of a herd. If this seems nakedly arrogant, call us "flawed protagonists." Every person who has ever started or helped start a business suffers from the same flaw.

◆ Today (Day 16), the radio update said the Wisconsin seat of government had relocated to a naval vessel in Lake Michigan. Planning was underway to fold the state government into a Midwestern super-authority to better coordinate resources in the region. This made a lot of sense as there was a massive duplication of disarray among the dysfunctional state governments and military commands.

Martial law would be formally declared across the country on Monday. Guard troops of all branches plus state and local law enforcement would be federalized. If there were protests about the suspension of state's rights, we didn't hear about it from the government run radio update.

In international news, the Vatican (as was all of Rome) had been declared lost. A different kind of mass was being held in St. Peter's Square now.

The military command channel was now joined with the public safety dispatch channel on the police scanner. A few of the tactical channels were patched together as well. What we heard was not promising.

In the evening, the safe zone at Chippewa Valley Regional Airport was declared closed to new refugees. Patrols outside the defensive perimeter were stopped. There was no need to go out looking for the enemy any more. The enemy came to them.

The defensive line roughly followed the airport's own preexisting fencing. The chain link would not hold for very long when hundreds let alone thousands of undead began pressing in on it. Concertina wire added to the fence was a waste of good concertina wire. The undead would be unfazed by cuts but perhaps might be caught up in it long enough to be shot. Soldiers manned barricades made variously of sandbags, concrete barriers or both. This was a waste of time. Zombies don't shoot back but could swarm around and over low defenses of this sort.

A different kind of enemy means different kinds of defensive measures. The defenders of Chippewa Valley Regional weren't equipped nor did they have time to erect a proper defensive line. It could be a slaughter in the making.

◆ On Saturday (Day 17), Ruth Ann and I couldn't resist temptation any longer and the hypocrisy was palpable. Archimedes had it wrong. He should have said,

"Give me a desire strong enough and a rationalization on which to base it and I will move the world."

Three of our neighbor's homes were open to nature, having already been violated by the looters we dispatched. For safety's sake, we decided to visit only the Olson house because it was closest. We didn't know the people well, but they were neighbors, right? And their house was already broken into, right? Bottom line, we were sure *we* wouldn't shoot at *us* like *we* shot at five men for doing almost the same thing *we* were about to do now.

Both of us armed, we drove the car around the corner to our neighbor to the east. Ruth Ann stood watch while I searched the home. In retrospect, I was foolish in that I just walked around normally inside the house, revolver still in my pocket. We hadn't seen yet how deviously a "dumb zombie" could hide. I found a number of blankets, bed sheets, bungee cords and other, what I would consider practical, things. I noted that the previous looters had torn apart our neighbor's entertainment center. With them dead, there was an Xbox sitting idle somewhere. There were some dry and canned goods left, which I also took.

We spent much of the rest of the day checking and rechecking inventories and mechanical systems. Ruth Ann drilled me on handling our various weapons. She took apart all four firearms for cleaning, oiling where necessary and reassembly. Ruth Ann also thoroughly tested the "new" rifle. She said it might be a more convenient weapon for me to use than her own hunting rifle as hers was bolt action and this one was semi-automatic.

The radio update said an invasion of Door County had begun. Door County is a spit of land sticking out into Lake Michigan. Surrounded on three sides by the lake and even further south by a river system, it had a relatively narrow entrance.

Starting with Washington Island at the northeast tip of the county, Army and Marine Corps units are going to go door to door combing every inch of ground heading southwest like squeezing a tube of toothpaste. Their aim is to leave no undead or infected person behind their advancing line.

◆ The radio broadcast on Sunday (Day 18), gave an update on the progress of the Washington Island campaign. It said that despite slow progress initially, the military was adapting and developing more effective tactics for dealing with this new type of fight. Our forces had control of the Washington Island Airport and were working to improve its capabilities. The commanders on the ground believed the entire island would be secure enough by the end of the next day to begin construction of refugee facilities.

Refugees still on the move were now warned away from safe zones and advised to seek the best hiding positions they could find. Safe zones were in fact attracting masses of undead. Zones without protective terrain were in increasing danger of being overrun. With operations now underway to completely disinfect islands and peninsulas, staying put (if relatively safe to do so) was increasingly a better option.

A new segment was added to the broadcast: advice. If the phone systems were working, it might have been a call-in show. The progression of the sickness was discussed as well as purifying water and best practices for killing zombies. Tips about zombie behavior were given.

Interestingly, the advice on the best places to seek refuge included being in a concrete structure far from a river or lake and not near major highways. In fact, structures of any kind near major highways were to be avoided because they were easy routes for mindless eating machines to follow. The dead were massing in larger and larger numbers. Shorelines were to be avoided because they were obstacles and caused the dead to bunch up. A concrete structure in the middle of nowhere was best.

Like right here at home.

Ruth Ann and I listened to our police scanner for long periods. Military and civilian law enforcement radio channels were trunked together to provide a common communication network permitting us to listen in to most traffic. The safe zone was heading downhill.

It was common now to hear weapons fire during transmissions. Sometimes we heard heavy machine guns. The strategy was still to defend the airfield to permit the commencement of evacuations. Tactics improved a bit but the defensive perimeter was simply too long for the forces they had. Helicopter gunships began operations at the airfield. Ruth Ann and I could see moving shapes above the field in our binoculars when we looked east from our roof. That evening as the sun was setting, we saw lines of light extend from points in the sky which raced to the ground.

◆ On Monday (Day 19), the news from Door County was good. Supplies from ships in Lake Michigan and hence out to the Atlantic were being ferried into the small harbor facing Rock Island. Construction of the first "truly safe" large refugee center in the Midwest had begun. The full-scale invasion of Door County proper was started. Because the area had been lightly populated to begin with, and with improving tactics, casualties among our troops was said to be minimal.

The Federal government finally declared martial law as expected this day. Seven states including Wisconsin were collapsed into the Midwest Administrative Zone. Wisconsin's controversial governor was finally out of a job. Running the Administrative zone was a military function.

The Air National Guard and civilian volunteer pilots started airlifting refugees out of Chippewa Valley Regional. It was clear the safe zone was going to fall. The only uncertainty was if its defenders could hold it together long enough to get everyone out.

Helicopters brought in a newly developed adaptation to this new type of enemy: the portable pillbox. Recognizing the crudeness of the zombie assault and that all immobile defensive positions will ultimately be overrun, the devices are portable steel boxes carrying an enormous amount of ammunition feeding a light weight battery operated Gatling gun, the GAU-19.

These were the same guns, but mounted on helicopters, that shot so quickly they made the continuous streams of light we saw last night.

The pillbox had a hook assembly on top. When the gun jammed or ran out of ammunition, a helicopter came along and whisked it away. If the box was overrun, the gunners were safe inside out of arm's and harm's reach. A rescue helicopter 'simply" needed to sweep away any ghouls covering the hook assembly which could be snagged if the box was upright or on its side.

Simple, safe and effective.

And in too short of supply. Exotic weapons such as these Gatling guns had to be spread across the country. No new ones were going to be made for a while.

I had an idea today to allow Ruth Ann and me to remain in contact with one another if we were separated (but in or near the house). Having walkie-talkies or those little FRS radios would have been better but as a Secretary of Defense once said, "You go to the zombie apocalypse with the tech you have not the tech you want." Of course Donald Rumsfeld didn't say exactly that, but the meaning is similar.

I took one of the Raspberry Pi's out and set it up to be an email server on our house network. Now, all of our WIFI devices including our phones can send and receive email as long as the device is connected to the house network. This was the first email system I'd been on since the early 1980's where I was confident of not receiving any messages from the widows of deposed oil ministers or persons with an overly large interest in my male parts.

◆ On Tuesday (Day 20), things were terminally grim at the safe zone at Chippewa Valley Regional Airport. Over our police scanner we heard that evacuations continued by plane until it was unsafe to operate aircraft from the main runway for fear of actually ramming undead walkers on the field. Another defensive line closer to the river was organized. Those remaining in the zone were ferried across the Chippewa River to farms on the other side. Evacuation by helicopter continued from the farms. When the last civilians had been airlifted out, a convoy of trucks and Humvees carrying the remaining troops and portable equipment slipped onto Wisconsin 29 and left the area.

Our police scanner was quiet after that. As far as Ruth Ann and I knew for sure, we were the last humans in this part of Wisconsin. We didn't do much of anything today other than listen to the scanner even after it went silent. We were depressed. We argued about nothings. We spent the remains of the day in different parts of the house.

◆ It is Wednesday (Day 21). We found out today where the next capital of the United States of America will be. Puerto Rico. And like the abandoned District of Columbia, Puerto Rico still won't get to be a state.

According to the national section on today's broadcast, a task force comprised of much of our country's returning European, African and Central Asian based forces have converged on the island's eastern end along with forces already to sea in the Atlantic.

There was no activity anywhere on our police scanner today. There were still digital bursts happening up in the ham radio bands but we had no way of knowing where in the world they came from or what they said.

We felt very alone today. Perhaps more so than any other day described in this book. While the Chippewa Valley Regional camp existed, it was like they were neighbors just over the hill and through the dale. We couldn't see them but we knew they were there. Now they're gone.

It wasn't shocking that the safe zone had failed. Never the less, that it *had* failed was a big blow.

◆ Hippies and liberals had an age old question answered today, Thursday (Day 22). During the international news segment of the daily update we learned that North Korea nuked Seoul, South Korea and then invaded their neighbor. The question that had been answered was "What if you threw a nuclear war and nobody showed up?"

North Korea's use of a nuclear weapon evoked no response at all. If, by "no response," one overlooks the opening of the border for the undead to go north. There hadn't been a single case of infection in the isolated north until they figured they would seize the opportunity to grab the south. We can be certain that the results were not what the dear leader had in mind.

Troops in Puerto Rico were finding rough going in trying to disinfect an island of more than three million people. Puerto Rico had forewarning of the outbreak so relatively few cases developed there.

"Relatively few" in this case meant only a fifty percent mortality rate compared to more than ninety percent in other densely populated areas. Isolating living humans long enough to ensure they were not infected grew to be one of the force's largest tasks.

Closer to home, our forces were making steady progress through the lightly populated area of northern Door County above Sturgeon Bay. Reaching Sturgeon Bay would be a milestone as the county is split in two there by a natural waterway and canal. Once Sturgeon Bay was secure, more than a hundred square miles of beautiful land would be available to host refugees.

Closer to home there were no sounds emitted by the police scanner again today. Ruth Ann and I were resigned that we would not be hearing anything more from it until Johnny came marching home again.

Would we still be alive to hear it?

We took stock of our supplies and situation feeling the strong tug of self-doubt. Certainly, there was no alternative now but to stay put. Supplies were fine, water and electrical systems were working. Hell, we had some bargain basement DVDs still in shrink wrap and dozens of books we hadn't read.

And we had each other.

All day.

All night.

We were sick of each other frankly.

◆ On Friday (Day 23), the weather continued its inexorable march towards deep freeze. We didn't mind too much as we had a constantly livable temperature in the basement and some electricity to run small heaters. That and plenty of layers kept us comfortable.

The radio informed us that our troops had reached Sturgeon Bay. To its northwest, disinfection of Door County was complete within a high degree of confidence. Between Sturgeon Bay and Washington Island, refugees from the greater Lake Michigan area could start settling in.

Ruth Ann brought up an interesting point this evening.

"I think when the plague is over the country will be more Republican," she said.

"Seriously, that's what you're thinking about? Zombies prefer the taste of liberals?" The freakishly tall anorexic blonde occasionally on Fox News had actually said this early on.

"I am being serious. Look, the higher the population density like in a city, the higher the death rate. If it is true that cities lean more Liberal than rural areas, then percentagewise we're losing more Democrats than Republicans."

She continued, "It is going to change Congress completely! Let's say New York loses ninety percent of its population but Wyoming only loses twenty because there is nobody there anyway. Wyoming's Congressional delegation is going to be larger relative to New York's than it is today."

It was then I smelled the aroma of Denny and Meg's prize winning "herb."

I hadn't touched the stuff and wouldn't be going to. Like all 'modern" Presidents, I had tried marijuana in college. In fact, I tried it really hard. In the end though the stuff just made my skin crawl.

I kept Ruth Ann company but from across the room so as not to pick up a contact buzz. There was enough skin crawling outside, I didn't need any in here too.

I did help Ruth Ann polish off the last of our Oreos.

◆ Nothing much happened for the next few days. We did maintenance around the house, watched our surveillance system and spent a good deal of time on the roof. The greenhouse smelled really “normal”. Nothing had changed inside that enclosure and that was comforting.

On the radio it was announced that the remains of the nation of Japan was now sea based. Not much else was said about conditions around the world.

Ruth Ann observed that either they didn’t know what was going on (which would be bad) or they didn’t want to tell us (which would also be bad).

The same could be said about conditions in the other Administrative Zones. Reports about anywhere except this area were few. On the plus side, there wouldn’t be any of the rumors like such and such amusement park in California was still operating causing people to trek across the country at great risk to themselves for no actual gain.

One ray of sunshine: It was now accepted as fact that the virus could not live airborne in freezing temperatures. For the remainder of the winter season, infection could only happen by bite or scratch.

◆ On Tuesday (Day 27), it had been a week since we picked up a signal on our police scanner. We hadn't been away from our property in quite a while and cabin fever had definitely set in. We wanted to see what was going on beyond our own horizon.

We made a plan to visit a nearby medical clinic to see if there were any supplies we might be able to take. My rationalizations had progressed to the point that it wasn't looting unless you were taking something from an actually living person. This way we could feel good about ourselves as we committed larceny and also feel good about ourselves for having killed four men almost two weeks before.

There was an enormous warehouse distribution center a few miles in the other direction. It would be nice to visit there too but the risks involved seemed too great for just Ruth Ann and me. The company that owned it was famous for never having a floor walker around when you needed one to help you find something. Ruth Ann and I both wondered how many ghouls could be found walking the warehouse's aisles now. We weren't in that dire a need for the beef jerky that would almost certainly be found there but the building supplies would have been nice.

The last time either of us had left the immediate area of the house, Ruth Ann had gone alone to get ammunition. That was ages ago when there were still living people around. We didn't want to risk leaving the house empty back then.

Now, with zombies found right outside, we actually felt safer both being away. We had a good solid house and watch zombies to keep people from casually wandering around trying doors. Besides, it would be too dangerous now for one person to go into a building without someone else covering them.

We packed up the Volvo and watched the cameras for a few minutes. Seeing nothing stirring I lifted the garage door while Ruth Ann pulled the car out. I locked up and we started on our way. We decided to avoid the main road and head to town the back way.

We didn't get very far before we came upon a two car wreck on 10th street just over a hill. We had been driving slowly so stopping before joining the wreck ourselves wasn't an issue. I never got why characters in zombie books were always speeding from place to place often getting into wrecks of their own making. With no zombies behind us, the only possible danger was in front. Why hurry into it?

We scanned all around us while Ruth Ann idled. From where we were, it wasn't clear there was a way through but it was clear there was movement inside one of the cars. To go forward we'd have to get a better look. I pocketed the revolver and took our crowbar. After zipping up to leave the warmth of the car, I stepped outside.

The vehicle closest to us was an empty pickup truck, driver's side door open. It had partially crossed the yellow line and crashed the driver's side corner of another pickup. It seemed everybody around here drove pickups. Some pickups were working trucks, hauling what they were intended for. Most though were just shiny toys.

In this case, the proverbial shiny red truck had a dull red to black interior coating of dried blood. With my crowbar ready to jab through a skull, I looked into the open door. Apart from the caked blood there was a tennis shoe, incongruously clean and appropriate for a teenage girl on the floor of the driver's side but nothing else.

The other car involved in the collision, another pickup, was an older model that was clearly a working truck. What had formerly been the working man that worked it was still inside seat belted with its windows rolled up. Clearly the temperature swings inside the car had not been kind. The rotted putrid hulk banged on every accessible surface keeping its eyes riveted upon me. With its windows rolled up there was only the dull banging and muffled moaning to be heard even from a dozen feet away.

Fortunately, zombies don't operate seatbelts or door locks; the ghoul wasn't going anywhere. I shifted the shiny red truck into neutral. The hardest part of shoving the truck backwards into the ditch on the side of the road was getting it over the road's crown. That and ignoring the raging zombie behind me. In short order the road was clear. As we drove past I half expected the other truck's driver to twist his head right around like Linda Blair in the Exorcist. It didn't happen.

We passed a large dairy building where cows came to get milked. There were no animals in sight. In fact, we hadn't seen any of the cows, horses, goats or even llamas that we usually saw along the road. On the exterior wall was sloppily painted

"God forgive me"

The screen door and interior door to the nearby house were both busted down.

After the local elementary school there was a dense crop of trees close to the road on either side. Ruth Ann didn't feel comfortable heading into it. She nosed in, far enough to see another wreck just around the bend in the road.

We backed up and went through the elementary school's parking lot side stepping the blocked bend in the road. The parking lots of the elementary school, high school and the middle school I was preparing the Raspberry Pi's for, were in disarray. Things were not looking good.

We turned left to get back to US 12 passing several houses that were boarded up. It was impossible to tell if anyone was inside. One home had burned to the ground. Near it lay decomposing corpses. One was headless, the other missing limbs.

Left again onto 12 we wanted to complete the loop back towards our house by stopping at the medical clinic just east of us.

As we made the turn we saw several statue like ghouls snap their heads in our direction. Immediately they began to move towards us. We easily opened up the distance even going as slowly as we were.

From where we were we could see about a thousand feet down the road in the direction of the clinic and home. We quickly determined we would not be stopping for supplies.

Dozens of walking dead, were in sequence, becoming aware of us and beginning to shuffle towards the Volvo.

"Doug, what do we do?"

"Go slow, don't panic. Seriously, slow down!" I said urgently.

"What?"

"Slow down! Put the car in low gear – we'll push through them!"

Our car was of the four-wheel drive variety. I knew from seeing enough deer strikes on the local news that if we panicked and sped up we would disable the car and die.

We saw each and every face that still had one. We saw the missing limbs, the ripped bellies with no intestines to fall through. We saw the gouges, the tears and bites. We heard the screaming, moaning, whines and wails. The pounding on the windows was worst with mangled heads pressed against the glass.

We kept moving at a slow and steady pace. We slowly knocked some over that fell like the last bowling pin to go down on a lucky strike. We drove over them. We dragged some until they wore away on the pavement. We didn't stop.

We didn't stop until we got home.

We spent the rest of the day washing the car with a pressure washer and dilute bleach. The car's finish might suffer from the bleach. Might not. We didn't know. We didn't care.

◆ Day 28 is lost to both Ruth Ann and I. All we remember about this day is sleeping a lot and the radio updates which included information that would change our lives forever.

Down in Puerto Rico things had come to a standstill. Now, all efforts were being put into holding the ground already gained (which wasn't much) while systematically sealing all sewers and storm drains. Too many recurrences of outbreaks were being caused by undead rising from underground tunnels in areas already thought disinfected.

Troops moving southwest in Door County were halted too after isolating the larger town of Algoma.

Much of rural Wisconsin is on well and septic, as we are here at the house. However, even small towns had storm water runoff tunnels and larger towns had sewer systems. Any underground passageway that could not be welded shut had to be blocked by detonation or other immovable means. Potential flooding in the future and even having to find safe alternative means of waste disposal was easily more bearable than undead popping up again today.

Ruth Ann and I were comforted by the subtext. Experience and knowledge was being shared at a national level and tactics continued to evolve and improve.

The big news, what made this day's update so memorable, is that massive hordes had begun their march out of the greater Chicago-land area. With all food consumed or converted into their own kind, seven million undead split into two groups called Chicago A and B. Four million were headed to Wisconsin.

"What can that possibly look like? How can anything survive?" Ruth Ann said.

"I don't know. The plague of locusts from the Old Testament? Herds of bison in the early days on the prairie? I don't know. I hope we don't find out."

◆ Go figure it was Halloween night (Thursday Day 29) when we had our first trick-or-treaters. Ruth Ann and I were buttoned up for the night. We were upstairs in the blacked out kitchen. The room was dimly illuminated only by a laptop and a hand cranked LED camp light on its lowest setting. The live security DVR was full screen. Our police scanner was on low volume but was silent as it had been for days.

Since our aborted trip to town, Ruth Ann and I hadn't ventured outside much and were spooked by any sound or perceived movement. We were just beginning to come back to ourselves putting some grim detachment between us and the things out there.

I was leaning against the counter; Ruth Ann was at the table.

"Doug!" she said. "Look." I quickly stepped over to her. The DVR was in its eight camera view. Each side of the house has two opposing cameras. They are oriented so that the walls of the house are just visible to one side with a wide field view of the lawn to the other.

There they were.

A tom turkey and five hens moved with purpose to the northwest. They didn't stop here and there to feed like I have seen them do when I drove past them a million years ago. I mentioned this to Ruth Ann. She said, "They're not scanning side to side. They are moving away from something behind them."

Then we could see a figure slowly walking at the limits of the IR illuminator of camera three (northeast view on the eastern face of the house). With each step it became better lit. Then we could see it in the second northeast view, camera six. Its arms hung loosely at its sides. Its head angled slightly down and was canted at an odd angle. We could see it wore a flannel shirt under an open down vest. Other than not being dressed for the weather and its odd posture and gait we could see nothing amiss. The former person looked fine. I felt let down.

It continued slowly to the northwest. Then a woman came into view heading the same way. It was a mess. Its forehead was caked darkly and its hair was matted on the left side. Its head was turned sharply to the left and up. As it walked closer to camera six, I clicked to make that camera full screen. Its face was oriented square to the lens. Its mouth was open, jaw slack. Dark stains were obvious from its mouth down its chin, torso, sleeves and hands. Its eyes glowed white in the infrared light.

I no longer felt let down.

◆ We sat in stunned silence. We had driven through a mass of undead just the other day but this was different even if much less dangerous. While the corpses we passed in the car and even bumped into were horrible, we were focused purely on escape. Now, watching the undead pass slowly in black and white silence one by one we were focused exclusively on them.

I felt Ruth Ann's hand take hold of mine. I could feel her pulse, maybe it was mine I don't know. We just sat there watching as it passed under the view of camera six. With a click of the down arrow, camera five looking northwest showed the man disappearing into the night followed by the woman, its head almost looking back at us.

The cameras had audio too but we could listen to just one at a time. Full screen on camera five we heard just light wind noise. Suddenly there was a low thud, but no source in view. I selected the all-camera view again and saw a big shape getting unsteadily up from the ground on camera six. It had hit the low enclosure that protected the top of our water well. There was movement on all four cameras with easterly views now.

The creatures were heading in the same prevailing direction, trailing the turkeys. I said quietly to Ruth Ann that they looked like they were exhibiting a flocking behavior. I remembered a graphics paper from the late 1980's describing self-organizing groups of individuals. A demo of the algorithm in the paper was called "Boids." Individuals in a flock exhibit both attraction to and avoidance of the other individuals.

We actually saw it happen when a child with one arm missing at the shoulder passed in front a man with a gaping hole where his guts should have been. The man slowed slightly. His head tracked the motion of the girl as he plodded in his original direction. As the dead child passed, he picked up his jerky pace again veering to the girl's direction.

In the infrared light more and more creatures filtered into view. Like coming through fog, at first they were indistinct.

Their image grew clearer as they staggered closer. One face was familiar.

The creature was in a ripped nightgown with its mutilated hips and midriff showing. The tears extended upwards showing its rib cage where its right breast had been.

"Doug, is that Charlotte Krause?"

"Who is Charlotte Krause?"

"Babe. Babe Krause. She owns the yarn store. That's her. I know her."

Ruth Ann's eyes narrowed. I could see anger on her face. These fucking things were here at *our* house. People we *know*. My eyes were also fixed upon the screen. I didn't know Babe Krause personally. Never the less, the corpse walking before us was part of our world.

Can I say the dire peril in which the human kind found itself just "became personal?" It is a cliché, but, yes. I can. Piece by piece the man whose world view was "People suck," was disappearing. The detached technologist who processed nameless and faceless people as so many ID numbers, who helped create massive systems to buy and sell them down the river without them knowing was suddenly becoming aware of the value of just one soul.

Ruth Ann was always my connection to the human race. She cared. She nurtured. Good thing she shot stuff too or we'd have been screwed from the start.

The point is I assumed she would be *more* troubled being so much more in tune with human connection. It turns out my wife's reaction headed in the other direction. As she watched her former friend head hungrily, vacuously and soullessly into the night, she became hardened.

As she grew more determined that we survive, I grew more accepting of the idea of helping others do the same. In a way, as in so many ways, we both grew on this awful night.

Mixed in with the wind noise we could hear many different unintelligible sounds emanating from the creatures. Some were monotonic. Some rose and fell in pitch. Some sounded wet while others rasped dry. There were long gutturals and short chuffs. There was no uniformity except in that none sounded entirely human.

After a while, Ruth Ann turned off the audio. Thankfully we could not hear so few of them through our walls and windows. We watched until we were stiff and our eyes burned. None of the creatures seemed to know we were here.

Our tea had long gone cold and went unfinished. We slept uneasily on our comfortable couches under piles of blankets in our well-appointed living room with a large flock of undead flowing slowly past us. The contrast was uncomfortable.

◆ When I woke up on Friday (Day 30), Ruth Ann was studying the laptop screen.

"There's still one outside. He's just standing in one spot like the first ones we saw in town."

In daytime, the cameras showed a color picture as opposed to night's black and white. The creature stood motionless to the northwest near the Boetche's house.

"How long has he been like that?"

"It. It's been like that for twenty minutes. There's coffee for you."

I like my coffee cold. The Keurig machine we have consumes all the watts generated by our rooftop panels when it brews so we used it carefully. The power consumption of the machine wasn't going to be a concern much longer though. We'd be out of coffee tomorrow. Then it would be only tea. We had a lot of bulk tea.

The dead guy was stock still as I continued to watch. Our view was mostly of his back. He stood in a droopy way. His head was down. From this distance he could have been a stoner listening to the national anthem at a baseball game. He had on a light jacket, an arm in one sleeve over one shoulder. The other end lay limply down his back. Still consistent with the stoner image I thought dryly. His pants legs were bloody though.

We put the security DVR into playback mode. I stopped first on last night's second creature, the woman that looked right up into the camera lens. "It's looking right at the IR LEDs and paid no attention to them. She kept on walking," I said.

"Does that really tell us much?"

"Maybe they can't see infrared or maybe they weren't cued into the illuminators because they were stationary."

"Don't all the zombie books say they see heat?"

"Pretty much."

"Doesn't infrared look warm?"

"Yeah."

"So maybe they don't see heat, or they do see heat but are triggered more by motion."

"Or maybe the zombie books are full of shit. How can a virus instantly give dead people super hearing and vision?"

"How can a virus make dead people rise?"

"Good point."

Debugging computer programs actually isn't that hard though most programmers suck at it. The key is careful observation, formulating a testable hypothesis, performing tests and observing the results.

If we were going to live though this it would be because we thought things through, I believed. I can laugh at this remarkably naïve view now but I was sure of myself then.

"We can test their night vision," I pronounced. "I have spare IR emitters that could easily run all night on some AA rechargeables. We can Velcro the setup to a tree branch so it sways in the wind like we did with the fake laser scopes. If more creatures walk by tonight and get excited then we know they can see IR."

"How fast are they? To tell you the truth I wasn't all that cued in on details when we were in the car." Ruth Ann said.

"Me neither. We can measure them just from the video time codes we already have. Take some screenshots of them walking. We'll go outside and stand where they were and measure. It won't be super accurate but we can average a few measures together."

"By "we" you mean me, right?"

"We both better go to cover each other. I'll bring a tablet to view you through the cameras and do the timing."

"OK"

"What about him?" I said pointing at the laptop.

"Shoot him first; answer questions later." Ruth Ann said.

“Can we avoid guns? Every zombie book says they’re attracted to noise.” This was true, every fictional and nonfictional account said gunshots were like dinner bells.

“By “we” you mean me again?” she ribbed. “I’ll try the bow but we’re both bringing firearms.”

◆ When it was time to take care of business we watched the all-camera view for about ten minutes. We flipped through the audio channels and heard nothing but wind noise. The stoner was unchanged. Ruth Ann attached her recurve hunting bow to its sling. Four razor tipped broad head arrows hung at her hip. We agreed that if she didn't drop the stoner in two arrows we'd risk a gunshot. Slung on her back was our carbine. She held a spare clip in her coat pocket.

I had asked her if I shouldn't go outside with the long rifle since I'd be further away. She looked at me, picked up the snub nosed revolver intended for in-home defense, checked its load and handed it to me. "Okaaaaay, there's a vote of confidence," I thought to myself.

I was also armed with a ten-inch Android tablet tuned into the house security DVR. I wasn't sure how far WIFI would reach outside so I wouldn't be venturing too far away. I did not want to give up the security of the all-camera view.

I made for the heavy sliding glass door at the back deck. Ruth Ann stopped me by saying, "We can't lock that from the outside. Let's use the front door."

"What if we get locked out?"

"Don't" she said. "Bring your keys. The chances of being locked out are small compared to the risk of one of those things getting inside the house through an open door."

She was right. We both took our keys and went to the front door. Looking at the tablet's screen, all cameras showed clear except for the stoner. Ruth Ann silently undid the lock and hasps. With a nod from me she quietly opened the door. "He's still there," she whispered, but I could see that on the tablet.

I nodded and made a "let's go" gesture. She opened the door wider. I checked the knob to make sure the door would lock behind us. We both were outside. I stood behind Ruth Ann and, realizing she was crouched low I quickly did the same. It occurred to me that I'm more Dumbo to her Rambo.

She motioned for the evergreen bush, a young tree actually, ahead and to the left of our driveway. We could see through the tree and knew it wasn't hiding anything. Almost winter, the grass was still short in our yard. Beyond the road separating us from the Boetche's backyard were wild grasses tall enough to conceal a body. All the trampled tall grass trails passed completely through. I was confident there were no threats there.

We crept low over to the evergreen. Ruth Ann pointed at me and pointed to the ground. This was to be my spot. My feed from the DVR was fine. I nodded to signal my understanding.

Ruth Ann continued crouched low. She crossed the road and reached the edge of the tall grass. She gave me a backwards glance. No threats on camera, I signaled thumbs up.

She crept into the tall grass, taking one of the trails made by the dead the night before. Crouched down, just her shoulders and head were visible. The stoner stood still, looking away from us.

Ruth Ann was about two thirds of the way through the tall grass making steady progress. She stopped. I heard a loud sustained moan like only the start of a pirate's "Arg!" Ruth Ann bolted upright and grabbed for something at her waist. I saw her hatchet rise up; I didn't even know she had it. She swung it down viciously. The pirate went silent.

The stoner snapped his head around, much faster than I anticipated. Turning, his whole front was covered in dried blood and he was missing all the skin on his face. Nose, cheeks, lips everything was gone. Just its teeth and eyes remained. Eyes fixed on Ruth Ann. I yelled. Ruth Ann dropped her hatchet.

The stoner was about 40 yards from Ruth Ann when it snapped out of its stupor. This was the far end of the range Ruth Ann said she was comfortable taking the shot with her bow. The stoner was on the move now. On the bright side, Ruth Ann would have the benefit of a shorter shot whether she used her bow or carbine.

I could see her left elbow move back to grab the grip of her bow. Then her right arm disappeared in front of her. I knew she was unclipping the bow from its sling. Her right hand shot down to her waist to her quiver. Up went an arrow then up went the bow bending as it rose. The creature had staggered more than five yards in the short time that had elapsed. This was faster than I expected, yet again.

It was leaning into its path, left arm out reaching for Ruth Ann. She took aim for what seemed like hours. At thirty yards she loosed. It was fucking gorgeous.

From where I was I couldn't tell if there was an arc to the arrow's flight but where it terminated its travel was certain. It passed into the creature's right cheek bone near its eye and nasal cavity. I saw the arrowhead glint in the sun poking out the base of the creature's skull as it twisted on its way down.

We both stood there. Presently Ruth Ann turned and walked upright back to the house. I intersected her path but before I could speak she said, "Don't say anything. Spray me with bleach water and let's get the fuck inside."

We didn't set up our experiments that day. Not testing vision or speed. It was enough to know the creatures could move much more quickly than we saw the night before. Indeed, we were pretty much cured of the desire to experiment at all.

We did not venture outside again that day. Instead, Ruth Ann sat quietly in the kitchen and slowly nursed some tea. We didn't talk till it was dark.

Finally she said, "I left my hatchet outside. And I want that arrow back. We don't have that many."

Before I could say anything she turned to me.

"There wasn't supposed to be anything in the grass, Doug. You said the trails went all the way through." Ruth Ann drilled her eyes into mine, they were puffy but I hadn't seen her cry.

"I know. I'm sorry. I played back all of last night. After we fell asleep one went in right behind another. The second one tripped on something, I saw it go down. The one in front continued on out of the grass making the trail look all the way through."

"When we were in the car I didn't look at them, I concentrated on staying moving and staying on the road. Today, today was different. There was no color in its skin. Their eyes are filmy like they had cataracts. There's no soul inside Doug. There's no person in there. They… They're monsters. They really are… monsters."

"It's OK honey. We'll be OK."

"Doug?"

Our faces were inches from each other's, I nodded.

"You have to learn to shoot better. You have to be able to cover me with more than a tablet."

"Yes dear."

◆ Ruth Ann took some antihistamines to help her sleep. She went to the living room to the couches. We didn't want to be too far away from each other. We believed our house to be a fortress, but it didn't matter. We needed to stay close to each other tonight.

I sat in the kitchen, angry that I had let Ruth Ann wander into a potentially lethal situation practically in our own front yard. I grabbed a pencil and pad and started thinking about what stuff I had and how I could apply it.

It occurred to me that, like it or not, our home is situated in a battlefield. While we had more surveillance capability than most homes, we needed to be able to see further out at night. It also occurred to me that there were no neighbors to complain and nobody to complain to if we started shaping the battlefield more in our favor.

Hell, if we could loot our neighbor's homes – I mean borrow from our neighbors, why couldn't we use their homes to help keep us safe?

Just before midnight, the police scanner stopped on an FRS channel and burped out some static. FRS is the Family Radio Service. These little, often cheap, handheld radios used to be available everywhere. The police scanner covers a lot of bands and stops only when it gets a strong enough signal. Unfortunately, that could be anywhere in a transmission, including its end.

The scanner is programmed to dwell on a frequency for a few seconds when it finds a signal on the assumption that someone would quickly respond. Someone did. I heard a crackly "OK" and then another burp of static. I turned off the scanning feature and stayed on this one FRS frequency but I heard nothing else until I went to bed.

Somewhere within a small number of miles of here, at least two people were alive. Since I heard nothing else for as long as I listened, I assume they were passing through. Still, it was nice to know we weren't alone for a few minutes at least.

◆ On Saturday (Day 31), Ruth Ann was up before me as usual. The events of yesterday seemed forgotten. The last of our coffee sat waiting for me on the table. As I reached for it, I reflected for a moment about how I was sad to see the coffee run out. I knew that millions maybe billions had already died and would continue to die of hunger, thirst disease, and the undead.

I wondered how a person could be empathic on a conceptual level and entirely self-absorbed about what's right in front them. I know I'm not the first to observe this. Didn't Stalin say "One death is a tragedy; one million is a statistic"? I wonder what Uncle Joe would say about billions.

"I saw deer wandering through at sunup," she said.

"Really? Turkeys the other night and deer this morning? Yet we didn't see any livestock when we went to town. I wonder which it is, do the dead eat animals or not?"

"I don't know but I do know how long one deer will feed us. We should take one if we can."

"You know how I just love to get up that early."

"You like to eat, right?"

"OK – we'll do it but only if there aren't any walkers around."

"Duh!"

Assuming no unwanted pedestrians tonight, we agreed we'd be ready to hunt tomorrow morning.

I told Ruth Ann about hearing a signal on an FRS band last night. She perked up.

"We don't have any kind of transmitter do we?"

"No. I ordered FRS radios from Amazon for that last delivery. They didn't make it. So, right, we have no way of initiating contact with anybody."

Some days back I had connected up one of the Raspberry Pi's to function as a local email server. We used the WIFI portion of our phones to buzz each other via email. That would do us little good trying to reach out to anyone else.

"We need some radios," she said.

"When do you think we should do it?"

"Do what?"

"Go to the building supply warehouse. They'll have that there and more."

"Yeah, and how many zombies? They were right outside the house Doug. We're not exactly a SWAT team that can go into a dark warehouse complex and come out alive. Put radios down on the "wants" list."

I did not dare mention that it was her idea to seek out radios in the first place.

Our list of "wants" wasn't terribly long but it wasn't empty either. Fortunately, the list of "needs" remained blank for now. That'll change, I thought to myself. I'd put coffee on the "needs" list or even on a "must have" list if we had one. As it was, Ruth Ann rolled her eyes at me when I put coffee on the "wants" list.

"I want more arrows," Ruth Ann said while looking at nothing in particular. "If the dead are close enough for a bow shot, we might be in bad shape if we fire a gun."

"I bought four boxes of them. They came in that last UPS truck."

"You bought the small boxes, six to a box. Plus I don't have as many broad heads as I'd like. You didn't buy any of those."

"Who would have thought you could buy an arrow that didn't come with an arrow head?" I said defensively. "Flynn up the street bow hunted. They're long gone. I don't think they'll mind if we "borrowed" some."

Flynn's house is the one north of the Boetche's. By now I was completely untroubled by any notion of a double standard. We had killed looters. Now borrowing a few things from absent neighbors seemed quite reasonable.

"Given how useful a bow is, don't you think he would have taken his?"

"No, they packed a few suitcases and got out on the first day of evacuations. Their kid needs medication. They weren't going to rough it."

We decided a trip to Flynn's house would be in order.

I brought up what I was thinking about the night before. We could use our neighbors' empty homes to extend our own safety.

"Let's try nailing one of those spare IR emitters up on Boetche's roof as a start. The infrared lights on our cameras don't reach too far. If we place an IR light source on their roof, we will be able to see all the way to their house. Their south side faces us so that little solar phone charger I bought last year can trickle charge batteries during the day and it'll shine all night."

"You can leave that sort of thing outside?"

"I have no idea. Can you spare a Tupperware container?"

"No… you can have a Rubbermaid"

I explained to Ruth Ann the holes I needed to get current from the little solar panel to a battery pack and out again to feed the IR emitter. We used some silicone caulk to seal the holes.

Before we headed out to the Flynn's, Ruth Ann went up to the roof to tend the garden. I topped off the water vessels in the house by running the pump. It didn't take very long to refill the bathtubs (one for gardening water, the other for a sequence of washing us, cleaning and a final reuse for flushing) and one of our collapsible five gallon containers (for drinking). I joined Ruth Ann on the roof. I gently swept a thin film of dust off the solar panels then checked their connections and mountings. While doing that I looked around for where I might put a WIFI access point to extend our range outside the house.

Ruth Ann and I took a good look at the Boetche's house and agreed that the top of their garage would be the best place to put the IR emitter. Unlike our garage which was tucked under our master bedroom, the Boetche's garage was semidetached. We'd need only a one story ladder which we already had.

For a while we looked at Flynn's house through our binoculars. There was a tree line beyond his house and a lot of space which we could not see. The house looked untouched. There was no reason to think otherwise. The group of creatures that passed through the other day left only the two stragglers Ruth Ann had killed so far as we could see.

We decided to visit Flynn's house first before putting up the IR emitter. We'd been close to Boetche's already and knew what we could see from our house was still clear. We decided we'd go alongside the Boetche's house and peek around front. This would give us a look up their street towards Flynn's at what we couldn't see from here.

We took along a crowbar and some duct tape to help with getting inside Flynn's. We armed ourselves as we did the day before with the exception of Ruth Ann's hatchet, which was still where she dropped it. We folded up a plastic garbage bag and put it into a backpack along with flashlights and some nitrile gloves. On the way back from Flynn's we planned to retrieve the hatchet and arrow left between our house and the Boetche's.

We made it to Boetche's house without incident. I got a look at the monsters Ruth Ann had dispatched the previous day. Continuing past them quickly was the only thing that saved me from retching from the sight and smell. We hugged the side of the house and stopped to regain our breath. We listened. Hearing nothing we inched to the front corner of the house. Peaking around, we could see the front of Flynn's house to the north. All was quiet. We stayed there to watch and listen for ten minutes anyway. This sort of slow movement with stops for watching and listening (and sniffing) was recommended in several of the zombie apocalypse survival guides we read. This advice was spot on.

We went back around the rear of the Boetche's house to head over to the Flynn's through their backyards. Staying in both house's backyards minimized the time we'd be exposed to ground we hadn't watched closely over the past month.

We reached the edge of the tall wild grass opening up to the Flynn house. Their raised deck was ahead of us, entering their second floor. The Flynn's stored their grill and other fair weather equipment under the deck.

I motioned to Ruth Ann to pause. We crouched down and watched. Something was swaying in the breeze in the shadows under of the deck. Except just then there was no breeze. Ruth Ann readied her bow. We crept closer.

We could see it now. What had apparently been a woman in a smart bloodstained suit rocked slowly back and forth shifting her weight from leg to leg. She had immense ugly slashes across what may once have been an attractive face. It appeared her throat had been ripped out. We heard it rasp, forcing air into its chest in an effort to bellow at us. As it started in our direction it tried to snarl but all that came out was hiss. Ruth Ann put her projectile through the thing's forehead at its hairline. The force of the impact snapped the top of the creature's skull clean off. It staggered but didn't stop. It closed the distance between us quickly again putting to a lie the claim our zombies were "slow." Ruth Ann notched another arrow and loosed it through the creature's gaping mouth. It dropped.

"Shot too high," Ruth Ann whispered. We remained crouched in the tall grass watching and listening for a few minutes. I had to pee. We had used two arrows. On the way back we'd want to retrieve these too.

We left the grass and made our way to the deck and up the stairs. We crouched at the sliding glass patio door and looked inside. Nothing appeared to be amiss. Using the duct tape, I taped a circle larger than the diameter of my fist and forearm near where the lock would be. With Ruth Ann keeping watch behind us, I smashed the glass through the center of the ring of tape using the pointy end of the crowbar. The outer glass broke nicely but the inner glass, without a border reinforced by duct tape made a lot of noise. Fortunately the intact outer glass muffled the sound to the outside of the house. Anything inside would now be aware of us.

Again we waited and listened. Nothing stirred. I gave a last look inside then reached in and undid the lock. I tried the door but it moved only an inch before stopping with a thud. The Flynn's had placed a wooden strip in the door's track to prevent what I was trying right now. Given the additional reach advantage of a break in the glass it was easy enough to flip the strip out of the track with the crowbar.

Upon opening the door, it chimed. Somewhere in the house an alarm status panel started beeping. If I didn't find the panel and disarm the alarm it was likely that a claxon would sound. We had heard the Flynn's alarm before when they set it off accidentally. It was designed to draw attention to the house, attention we did not want. If it was like our house's alarm system, I'd have less than 60 seconds to disarm it.

Since I didn't know their codes, I would have to find their alarm box and disconnect its battery backup. The power grid was gone so the system must be running off its lead acid battery. I bolted into the house to follow the sound. Ruth Ann raced up the deck stairs after me. Later, in the most loving way possible, she chewed me out for running headlong into a space we knew nothing about. I felt flush when I realized I could have been running into the waiting arm or arms of the undead.

Fortunately, the Flynn's house was truly vacant. I followed the beeping to its source; an alarm panel placed just like ours next to the door between the house and garage. But where was the battery? Unlike Hollywood computer geeks I can't just tap keys on the panel until I exclaim "I'm in!"

Like our house the laundry room is right next to the garage and, like our house, the alarm cabinet was in the laundry room closet. I opened the cabinet and removed one battery lead. No more beeps. After another moment's thought, I took the whole battery.

We next secured the deck door behind us and began our search of the house. We knew Flynn's home office was in the basement. That was our first guess as to where the bow and supplies would be found. This time Ruth Ann took the lead armed with her carbine. I pointed the flashlight from behind her. It would have been nice if we had a weapon mounted light. Put that on the list of "needs." Our caution proved unnecessary as the basement was clear.

Flynn's bow, a complicated and scary looking compound thing, was mounted on the wall. Below it, mounted vertically was a T-shaped contraption with a rifle stock. Flynn had a crossbow. All I knew about crossbows is that they looked really cool and that a Pope had outlawed them in the 12th century.

In the office closet we found three sealed boxes of five crossbow bolts each and one open box missing two bolts. There were also two boxes of a dozen carbon fiber arrows each and some supplies including more than a dozen razor sharp broad heads. We had found what we came for.

We didn't want to push our luck too much and went back upstairs to head home. On the way we stopped in the kitchen and pantry and found a supply of canned goods and non-perishables large enough to warrant a future trip back even after filling our pack. There was a large jar of instant coffee. I considered leaving it but only for a moment. Unlike before the war, instant coffee was now better than no coffee.

Our backpack full, Ruth Ann made her way down the deck's stairs and covered me while I closed and flipped the lock on the sliding door. Even with the hole in the door allowing ready access to the lock we knew the dead lacked the thought to make use of it. They'd just go through the door.

On our way back, Ruth Ann put on the nitrile gloves and pulled the arrows she'd expended out from their resting places and picked up her hatchet. It was disgusting but the woman I married was remarkable. We arrived back at our house without event. We left the garbage bag with the contaminated weapons out front. We brought the backpack in but didn't unpack it. Instead we set out with our ladder to the Boetche's garage.

We had the IR illuminator to set up along with its improvised power supply. I am sure we looked like idiots carrying a 10-foot ladder with ourselves laden with bows and guns stopping from time to time to look and listen. Fortunately there was no one there to snicker.

It was getting late. I was still on the roof finishing orienting the illuminator towards our house. There was a low beating noise; we froze.

"Doug, get down here we're leaving now!" barked Ruth Ann.

"Wait, listen. It's a helicopter!"

Quickly, out of the east three Blackhawk helicopters came zooming low. Two of them had weapons on little wings sprouting from their sides. The third had legs connected to soldiers dangling out of its sides. We were dumbfounded.

My first thought was that I didn't want them to shoot us like random water buffalo in a rice paddy (great movie). And, I didn't want to make it look like we were desperately in need of rescue. We had already said no many times to the National Guard. I did the only neutral thing I could think of.

I stood up straight and saluted.

As the helicopters passed I could see a lot of heads slowly turning to look at us. They may have been as dumbfounded as we were.

As we headed back to our house I said to Ruth Ann, "At least they weren't black."

"What?"

"Black helicopters, those were green."

"So?"

"In the movies bad things always happen when black helicopters are around."

"I see," she said.

It was just about dark and we were out of range to connect to the house's security cameras to help ensure we had no unexpected company. We left the ladder up figuring the undead couldn't make use of it. This allowed us to get back to the house sooner while there was still light.

◆ That night after buttoning up we had a good dinner including fresh salad from the roof and opened a bottle of wine. We were both overjoyed at seeing functioning troops again and at our success in locating some much needed supplies (bow supplies, food and coffee). I checked the security cameras and was pleased to see the new IR emitter on the Boetche's garage gave us a nighttime view all the way to their house.

We hadn't listened to the radio yet today so we tuned in to the update. A horde had finally come out of the Twin Cities. It crossed the river and was headed into Wisconsin rather than away. America's Dairyland was not catching any breaks. Karma no doubt, since the plague was a Wisconsin export.

The Twin Cities horde was estimated at two million. Add this to Chicago B and hordes in Wisconsin totaled six million walking dead.

The helicopters we saw were heading west to join what the authorities were calling a "thinning operation."

Dealing with a horde that numbered in the millions, wasn't as simple as going out there with guns blazing. Terrain had to work in your favor to cause the horde to bunch up. Sort of "would you mind standing closer together please so my weapons will be more effective?"

We were both curious if we could make out anything about where the helicopters were going or what they were up to. We bundled up as it was getting pretty cold at night. Bringing our binoculars we had a seat on the roof and looked west. In the dark under some cloud cover we could see flashes and glows of orange across a broad swath of the horizon. These filled enough of the horizon for us to know it couldn't be just the three Blackhawks we saw. There were other forces out there acting in concert.

We couldn't hear anything except the breeze. Using the binoculars didn't help. We could see only glows. Some changed suddenly brighter or darker others just glowed. We watched for a while but did not make out any details.

The faint sound of the helicopters came upon us. We could see three tiny dark holes moving against the glowing background. When they were no longer backed by the glowing horizon we couldn't see them at all but we could hear them getting closer. Soon we could see three sets of dim running lights blinking.

When they neared, two kept moving east. One circled slowly around the house.

It was close enough to be really loud. We didn't dare raise a rifle in their direction so Ruth Ann detached its night scope and raised just that to her eye. I knew that in their night vision gear we were probably the brightest thing for miles around. The helicopter made a complete circuit of the house and continued its way eastward.

Ruth Ann said the helicopter was marked United States Army and was one of the ones with the wings for weapons on its sides. The side doors were closed but Ruth Ann could make out the shape of the pilot examining us. Before they left, the pilot gave her a slow wave.

◆ We didn't go hunting on Sunday morning (Day 32), as we had hoped. On checking the cameras, in addition to many agitated dead, we saw something that rocked us back on our heels. There was a person lying propped up on both elbows on the Boetche's garage roof next to the IR emitter we put up the day before. He had pulled up the ladder we left standing.

We quickly dressed and rushed up to the roof with our binoculars, both the carbine and hunting rifle and Ruth Ann's bow. Immediately upon opening the roof door we could hear the dead bellowing. We kept out of sight. I poked up just high enough to look through the binoculars. Ruth Ann did the same through the hunting rifle's scope.

We counted a baker's dozen dead visible from our vantage point. Presently a fourteenth staggered into view from around the garage. Then a fifteenth appeared. And then still more. The person on the roof was doomed unless we helped.

The dead don't scream like people. There were almost no consonants in their noises, just long vicious vowels. The din was continuous with each individual pausing only to draw in a resupply of air to immediately force out again in the form of soulless scream. Even though it was cold, no steam came from their exhales. They were just as cold as the air they ejected.

Through our glasses we could see what looked like spit flying. It was probably bits of whatever was in their mouths because we've never seen them drink anything but blood. They grabbed at the air but could not gain purchase on the siding. Neither could they reach the garage's roof gutters. Even if they could they would probably just rip them down rather than be able to use them to climb up.

The person bundled up on the roof was safe for the moment if he could keep himself relatively calm and do nothing stupid. The thought of this reminded me of an old saying of something like "If you can keep your calm while those around you..." go nuts or something. I added silently "you must be on a roof surrounded by zombies."

"That's Ryan," Ruth Ann exclaimed.

"Who?"

"Ryan! Ryan Boetche. He used to mow our lawn for shit's sake."

"Oh yeah…"

Ruth Ann was about to shout out to Ryan but I stopped her.

"What are you doing?" I asked.

"What do you mean "What am I doing?". That's our neighbor's kid. We have to help him."

"Just invite him in? What if he's infected? What if he doesn't know he's infected?"

"What are you saying? We're not leaving him out there."

"I'm not saying that. I'm saying we have to think this through. We have to have a plan. We're alive because we think. If we want to stay alive we can't go off halfcocked."

"We have to let him know help is coming."

"And, we have to get him in on the plan as soon as we figure one out." We looked at each other. Then it hit me.

"Do you have your phone?"

"It's down stairs."

"Go get it. Get a tablet too. And put a small bottle of water in a plastic grocery bag, we still have some of those right? Who knows when he drank last? And an energy bar. But the bottle has to be small, OK?"

We both moved for the door downstairs.

"OK. What are you going to do?"

"I'm going to fly a care basket over to him."

"What?"

"You'll see."

◆ I rejoined Ruth Ann on the roof. She had what I asked for. I trailed behind me an Ethernet cable and held an old Linksys access point with its power brick. When I had taken the old blue box out of service it was configured as a bridge and none of our security settings had changed. The phone and tablet should simply connect. I plugged in the box and connected the LAN cable. Shielding the box from the sun, I confirmed the status lights looked good.

"Doug, what the hell are you doing?"

"Ryan is safe for the time being. We have to be able to talk to him without attracting the dead's attention."

"The phones don't work."

"They have WIFI. Remember the email server I set up? If we get him a phone hooked up to our network we can email him."

"How are you going to get him the phone?"

"I told you, I'm going to fly it to him. Trust me."

I ducked downstairs again and came back up with my hexacopter and radio controller. If you aren't familiar with hexacopters think "personal UAV."

I set it down.

"Put this, the bottle, a phone and the energy bar in the grocery bag and tie it shut." I handed her a note folded over with README written on the outside. She did as I asked while I prepped for flight. I took the bag and gave it a quick heft.

"No problem. It weighs less than my camera."

My hexacopter could carry a payload of a few pounds enough for a small DSLR and lens. I looped the bag's handles through the hexacopter's undercarriage and lifted off slowly. The bag remained attached and rose along with the hexacopter.

Ryan saw it immediately and got to his feet. The creatures were so engrossed in howling for Ryan's blood and banging on the garage that they didn't notice the hexacopter until it was over them. They reached up for it and bellowed louder but of course couldn't reach it.

I couldn't land the hexacopter because of the pitch of the garage roof. I hovered the drone a little above Ryan's head. He reached up and unhooked that bag carefully. I lifted the drone up higher and started it back to us.

He opened the bag. He read the note first (good boy), took the phone out, looked at it and signaled thumbs up confirming the phone was connected to our WIFI. The trip had taken only a few minutes but the hexacopter's batteries don't last long. I needed the thing for step two of my plan. On landing the hexacopter I put its batteries into a rapid power dump and recharge. I could trust them again in forty five minutes.

I tapped out an email:

"Sit tight. We need time to plan. Are you bitten or scratched or sick?"

I read it to Ruth Ann and sent it to the other phone. I told Ruth Ann, "You know we can't trust his answers. If he's scared he'll say anything."

"I know. We need a way to keep him isolated for a while."

We could see Ryan read the email and type a reply. In a few seconds my tablet buzzed with his answer.

"Tired thirsty hungry no broken skin not sick. Thank you so much!!"

I wrote back:

"Stay quiet and don't move. My helicopter needs 45 minutes to recharge. You'll be OK. We will come up with a plan."

He read the email and nodded back to us. He laid down again. I am sure the pounding on the garage walls and the dead's deafening howls made it impossible for him to go to a happy place.

◆ It didn't take Ruth Ann and me long to come up with an idea. We would make a diversion to give Ryan a chance to get on the ground and run. He could stay in our garage for a day to see if he got sick. If he did, we'd have to deal with it.

Ruth Ann and I put some blankets, a sleeping bag, change of clothes, food and water into our garage along with a spray bottle of bleach water. I released the garage door's hasps and reengaged the electric lift mechanism. We left him a tablet and its power brick so he could monitor the cameras, listen to music and even watch a movie for distraction.

Finally, we included both earplugs and a set of over-the-ear headphones. We had already learned that the dead can be loud enough to wake the living and then some.

We emailed Ryan our plan. We told him we were sorry we would not let him in directly and that staying in the garage for a day would be safe and relatively comfortable. He wrote back that he understood and our garage would be better than what he had been through.

While we waited for the hexacopter's batteries to recharge the banging and howling continued over at the Boetche's garage. By our count there were twenty-two zombies fixated on getting at Ryan. They looked as if they would climb on each other if they were packed densely enough. They lacked the cognitive ability to work together so without a crush of others, Ryan would continue to be safe. The thought crossed my mind that in the middle of a horde, even a second floor wouldn't be safe.

Finally, the battery recharge time had elapsed. We wrote to Ryan:

> *"We are ready to draw them off you. Wait for our signal. When clear, run to our garage. Don't trip on the body in the tall grass. Sorry again about quarantine – can't take chances. We'll open the door when you get close. You close it. Button is near inner door. Hang on to our phone, OK?"*

Ryan gave us the thumbs up. My drone lifted off. Slung beneath it was another light plastic grocery bag with our second phone in it. Its volume was turned up to its maximum and was playing MP3 files. Before you wonder, Barry Manilow and Barry White were far less effective in getting the ghoul's attention than B.I.G and Dr. Dre. With the phone on random play of what ever happened to be on it we couldn't pick and choose.

The dead didn't hear the music over their own screaming and pounding until the drone got close to them. Our location went unnoticed. I hovered above their reach buzzing back and forth until I had the attention of most of them. I slowly flew just ahead of them and drew more than a dozen towards Flynn's house. They moved like a spastic train. I had to loop back a few times to ensure that I continued to hold their attention while softer songs played.

I flew as far away from both Ryan and us as I thought I could safely fly and not lose control of the drone. I hit the "Hold Station" button on the remote control. The hexacopter would keep itself steady within a small radius of where I left it several feet above the reach of the monsters.

Ruth Ann started firing on the dead that I didn't draw away. She quickly downed the few on the south west side of the Boetche's garage. Ryan put our ladder down and started to descend. I ran downstairs to the garage with another one of our tablets so I could monitor the surveillance cameras. Our garage door area remained clear. Ruth Ann continued dropping whatever ghoul was closest to Ryan as he ran to us. On another camera I saw the dead that followed the hexacopter were on their way back towards the source of the louder noise, Ruth Ann's gunfire.

As Ryan reached our garage I opened the inner door and depressed the garage door button. As the door lifted I was once more thankful for the tax credit that allowed us to install our solar panels. I closed and bolted the inner door. I heard Ryan run into the garage and slam the button just on the other side of the wall from my head.

"Ryan?"

"Yeah."

"Strip out of your clothes and throw them in the corner. Spray yourself with bleach water and wash off. We left you clean clothes. I have to go back upstairs now. OK?"

I didn't wait for his answer.

◆ As soon as I got upstairs, I brought the drone back. The phone / decoy kept belting out tunes as the hexacopter bounced to a landing next to me.

"Is he OK?" Ruth Ann asked as she changed clips.

"He's inside," not actually answering the question. "How many things are left?"

"Look for yourself, they're right downstairs."

I looked over the parapet into the snarling faces of a dozen creatures. The stink, even outdoors was surprisingly bad. Some were rotted with tattered clothes. Others, like a kid no older than Ryan looked to be in great shape other than paper-thin ashen skin, broken jagged teeth and filmy eyes. It wore a University of Minnesota Golden Gophers jacket. Did the thing walk here from the Twin Cities?

They pounded and kicked the siding and garage door. They charged the house with all their weight rebounding with no apparent sense of the impact. A lot of good it would do them.

Ruth Ann handed me the carbine and made sure I had properly wrapped the sling around my arm. "Safety off?" she said.

"Safety is off." I flipped the switch, pleased that I remembered where it was.

"OK then, lean over the side and kill the fuckers."

I watched her mouth say those words and pictured them saying "I love you," even "I do," at our wedding. I couldn't believe I was hearing "kill the fuckers" come from my wife's lips. I considered for a moment that some of the creatures below had no lips at all anymore. They too had said "I love you" during their own now finished lives.

"Relax Doug. Remember what we worked on. Squeeze the trigger. Don't anticipate the recoil. Just let it happen."

I did as she said. The weapon discharged before I realized it. If the sling hadn't been wrapped around my arm I would have dropped the carbine over the side. A bullet tore through the Gopher's outstretched hand and pierced its brain.

"Good. Take your time. Breath. Do the next one."

I pointed the gun at the next closest monster, also right below me. This was a big burly man. One of the arms that reached up for me ended in ripped flesh and two jagged broken bones. As I squeezed the trigger it was shaking its head like a dog with a chew toy. My shot entered its temple and came out the other side. In going down, the big guy bowled over two ghouls next to him. My next shot entered one of the grounded creature's forehead just above its nose. Apart from rocking the creature's head backward there was no reaction in its face. It didn't grimace in pain, nor show surprise nor even close its filmy eyes. It just "stopped."

Ruth Ann put down her hunting rifle and fired our revolver. I kept firing as well. Our shots created a syncopated rhythm that I imagined could have been featured in one of the gangsta rap songs that had drawn the undead so effectively during our diversion to save Ryan.

Suddenly there was banging from the south side of the house. I went to it, leaned over the parapet, and was unexpectedly ten feet closer to two ghouls than I was before. These had climbed our deck and were pounding on and kicking our sliding glass door. I could see puss and goo left as ugly streaks and even face prints on the reinforced glass. The creatures faced straight ahead until I made a tiny noise in moving my rifle into position. Their hearing was quite intact.

I had been worried about this door as being our weak link. I realized now the stairs had to go. Maybe the whole deck had to go. It was not an acceptable risk to permit access to the glass door even if it was laminated in baseball bat rated plastic. Removing the deck would be for a different day. Right now I removed the threats on the deck with the carbine. The last shell ejected differently than the others. I recognized this as being out of ammo.

Ruth Ann had already used a speed loader and was on her second set of six shots. When I returned to the front of the house, Ruth Ann was holstering the revolver.

“Is that all of them?” I asked.

“No, there’s a couple more out front and there are more heading our way. I want to get some practice with the crossbow.”

Setting up the crossbow to fire was a multistep process involving feet, bending and cranking. Clearly this weapon could only be used at a safe distance as reloading is too slow to be useful in close quarters. The crossbow was so powerful that from our almost straight down firing angle the first bolt disappeared down the insides of the zombie. It was as good as lost. I sure wasn’t going to fish it out.

Ruth Ann just shrugged her shoulders and put down the crossbow. She supervised me reloading the carbine and I took down the remaining few at the base of the house. This left only those still heading for us from a distance attracted by the noise.

We crouched down and watched the ghouls heading towards us. They continued in our direction for a bit but seemed to lose focus after a while without continued noise and motion. This was the first time we witnessed what amounts to “undead attention deficit disorder.” Low temperature slows whatever passes for thought inside their minimally functional brains.

If they can see or hear you or if close, smell you, they’ll come after you relentlessly. If another ghoul is lashing out at something, ghouls nearby will maintain focus and be drawn in. But, if you had a good place to hide that gave them no further stimulus, the colder it gets the greater the potential they could lose interest. That does not mean they’ll wander off. They might enter a low power mode and just stand there. They can stand still far longer than a trapped person can wait.

Ruth Ann wanted more practice with the crossbow. She noisily loaded up another bolt and rose slowly above the parapet wall to take aim. A moment after she fired a creature heading away from us spun violently to the ground. In the time it took Ruth Ann to crouch back down behind the wall, the creature got back to his feet and continued walking in another direction entirely, a crossbow bolt protruding from the back of its shoulder.

Ruth Ann said, "I would need more practice with this before I'd really trust it." as she put down the crossbow. "At distance I'm not accurate enough with it yet. The feel is between bow and rifle. It's like trying to play tennis and then ping pong. It's too awkward for me."

"It was pretty exciting close up," I replied. "Termination with extreme prejudice."

"Yeah, that first shot probably stopped somewhere in the bastard's leg."

"You're more than welcome to look for it."

"No thanks. Let's get off the roof and check on Ryan."

We gathered our equipment and in two trips had the roof cleaned up.

◆ "Ryan?" Ruth Ann and I were at the door to the garage.

"Ryan?" Ruth Ann called again. There was no answer.

"RYAN?" we both yelled through the door.

"Here, yeah. I'm here." We heard him come to the door.

"Are you OK?"

"Yeah, I'm good. I had your headphones on. I never thought I'd see a movie again. Are they gone outside?"

"There are a few left but they lost interest in us." I said.

"Yeah they do that in the cold."

"Ryan, honey?" said Ruth Ann.

"Yes Mrs. Handsman?"

"Ryan, how did you get here?"

"I drove." Apparently even in the apocalypse you had to pull teeth to get information out of a teenager.

"We know that. We need to know where you came from and how you survived to get here."

"The Brute and I drove from the capital."

"You drove from Madison?" we were confused.

"No, from Sturgeon Bay. There are a couple of hundred thousand people in Door County now. It's the largest settlement in the Midwest."

We knew refugees were being collected in the safety of Door County but two hundred thousand people being the largest settlement in an area that encompassed Chicago, the Twin Cities and Milwaukee?

"What about the cities? What about the Twin Cities, Chicago? Is it as bad as the radio says?" Ruth Ann asked.

"Worse, Mrs. Handsman. Cities belong to the dead. I heard stories of people in tall buildings around the country that destroyed the stairs below them. They grow food on their rooftops and balconies. But that's it. Bigger the city, bigger the horde that's going to come out of it once they eaten everything they can find."

"Who is the Brute? Where is he?" Ruth Ann asked.

"His real name was Bert. He was regular Army. We drove together. I had my car and he drove his motorcycle. He scouted ahead so we could avoid getting stuck by wrecks."

"Where is he now?"

"He got eaten a couple of nights ago. He told me on the radio he saw some wrecks and was going to check them out. I said "OK". I followed behind him. I saw him skid out on some ice and he slid right into a dozen of those fucks. Excuse me Mrs. Handsman. He never had a chance. It happened just a few miles from here."

"Were you using little FRS radios, like walkie-talkies?" I asked.

"Yeah." That must have been the "OK" I heard. It was Ryan's last words to his partner.

"Mr. Handsman?"

"Listen Ryan it's the end of the world. You can call me Doug."

"OK. Doug?"

"Yes Ryan."

"Do you have any toilet paper in here?"

Ruth Ann and I looked at each other blankly. We stocked the garage with a lot of things, but no toilet paper.

"No, we forgot that. There is a box of paperbacks in there. You can rip out the pages. Start with 'A Clash of Kings.' Take out a garbage bag to throw your waste in. You'll only be in there for a day."

We figured we'd let Ryan do his business. We wanted to know why he left the safety of Door County in the company of a soldier but that would be another time.

◆ Ruth Ann and I went upstairs. She powered up the laptop and accessed the surveillance camera DVR. We could see several undead in the distance scattered in multiple directions. A couple of them were standing still. Frozen in place, it was as if they were hibernating. More were in motion. A few were still heading in our direction and some heading away.

The day's radio update brought detailed information about the horde that was moving east from the Twin Cities:

"the central axis of the horde follows Interstate 94. At noon today, the advancing face of the horde passed near Hammond and Baldwin Wisconsin. Thinning operations where local terrain is favorable will continue.

The next operation is scheduled to take place tonight along the Red Cedar River near Menomonie Wisconsin. All persons taking shelter in the area closest to the river or Lake Menomin are advised to relocate away from the waterfront.

All other persons are advised to seek or remain in the strongest shelter available. Persons camped on open ground or in woods are advised to flee northeast towards unpopulated areas. Unreinforced structures can be destroyed. If no suitable shelter can be found, seek high broken ground that is difficult to climb. Bluffs or promontories facing the direction of the oncoming horde are best.

Again, unreinforced structures such as residential buildings may not survive the crushing forces of a passing horde. You are advised to seek shelter on upper floors of reinforced commercial structures or apartment buildings. Destroy staircases below you.

If no suitable shelter can be found, seek high broken ground that is difficult to climb. Bluffs or promontories facing the direction of the oncoming horde are best."

"They will be here tomorrow afternoon," Ruth Ann said.

"We're built like a commercial building. In fact, the house is better than most banks. I think we'll be OK."

"Two million of those things. Why don't they just bomb them into the stone age?"

"The horde coming towards us isn't the only one around. I bet every metropolitan area spawned hordes that big. Or even bigger. The one out of Chicago is what, four million they said? I doubt we have enough men left, bombs, bullets, or fuel to kill them all."

"What are we supposed to do," Ruth Ann looked deeply at me.

"Us? We button up tight and keep our heads down. The rest of the country? I have no idea."

We spent the rest of the day doing chores around the house. Prewar chores like doing laundry were changed in that we used a washboard instead of the washer. We had new chores like refilling ammo clips and making sure anything with a battery was charged during daylight.

We chatted with Ryan a few times but he evaded our questions about why he left the safety of Door County. We did get an answer to something we were curious about. Why didn't the dead that chased him wander off once he was out of sight on the garage roof? His answer made perfect sense.

"One of them saw me get on the roof and came over. Once it started banging, more came. Every one that makes a commotion attracts more. Once they start banging they keep each other excited. That's how the hordes start out," he said.

A critical mass of zombies creates a sustaining reaction. We realized that even one sufficiently motivated zombie could potentially snowball into a horde the size of the one heading straight for us.

◆ Ruth Ann had fixed an early dinner of vegetarian chili with some re-hydrated beans and herbs from the roof. We were sitting down when we heard then felt a return of helicopters. It was unexpectedly loud. They must have been right outside. The security DVR displayed on the laptop on the table. Camera two showed a Blackhawk settling down near the back of the house.

We ran up to the roof. We arrived in time to see a crewman in a flight suit and an enormous helmet jump out of the chopper. He carried a black hard plastic case wrapped in shrink-wrap. In the distance, we could see the dead starting to converge on the giant green noise machine. We couldn't hear shots but every few seconds a corpse would be rocked backwards by an expert headshot. The crewman ran up our back deck stairs and placed his package near the heavy-duty door after kicking away the bodies of the dead zombies. He looked up at us peering down at him and returned the salute I had given the helicopter crews the night before. Apparently my gesture had made an impression. Just like that, he was off back to the Blackhawk.

The bird lifted off but stayed low and slow as it edged away from us. We realized they were leaving a noise trail heading away from the house to help draw creatures away from where they landed. A few hundred yards away they zoomed up and were gone.

We came down from the roof to retrieve the case. The deck door was a mess of streaks. We both put on nitrile gloves, opened the door and wiped down the case with disinfectant. I don't care what the radio said; I wasn't taking chances with our lives unnecessarily. We cut off the plastic wrap. A printed label was taped across the case's latch.

"By opening this case you acknowledge that it and its contents remain the property of the Department of Homeland Security and will be returned immediately upon request. Any unauthorized use of this equipment will be punished to the fullest extent possible under criminal law including but not limited to five years imprisonment and fines of not more than $250,000."

It was good to see our government still had its sense of humor.

We brought the case inside and locked up the deck door. We opened the case. Inside was a printed sheet on top of an instruction manual, which in turn rested on a Motorola tactical radio. The printed sheet said we were call sign "Christmas Tree." We would be contacted by "Lambeau Field" at 1800 hours, not too long from now. We were to use preset one. Preset two, we were instructed, was to be used only in emergencies. I wondered aloud if being surrounded by two million walking dead qualified as being worthy of preset two. There was also a power cord and what appeared to be an optional external antenna. It looked optional because there was an antenna looking thing already attached to the unit but I couldn't be sure.

We wiped down everything in the case with disinfectant. Looking at the back of the unit there was a receptacle that matched one end of the other antenna marked "External Antenna (Optional)." That settled that question.

We plugged in the unit but kept it off as we were unsure of its power draw (we found that later in the manual). We distractedly ate our dinner and waited for six PM to arrive. Just before six, we powered the unit up. A green two line LCD display glowed saying we were on preset one.

At the stroke of 1800 hours the speaker came alive.

"Lambeau Field calling Christmas Tree. This is Lambeau Field calling Christmas Tree, over."

"This is Christmas Tree. Can you hear us… over?"

"Affirmative Christmas Tree. Please state the last four digits of your social security number."

Huh?

"Why do you want my social security number?"

I told Ruth Ann that if they asked for a credit card I was tossing the radio off the deck.

"It is a formality Christmas Tree. We try to identify and keep track of survivors."

I gave them the last four digits of my national ID number.

"Thank you Christmas Tree. Is Mrs. Christmas Tree also with you?"

"Yes."

"Thank you Christmas Tree. Are you aware of any other survivors in your area?"

"Yes. We found the son of our neighbors across the road to the northwest. He is in our garage until we're sure he isn't sick."

"Thank you Christmas Tree. Please hold for your handler."

"OK. Can you stop saying thank you all the time? You sound like a cable company call center."

"Thank you Christmas Tree. One moment please."

A new voice came over the speaker.

"Christmas Tree, I will be your contact. You can call me Frank."

"Hi, Frank. Sorry about that call center crack. Mrs. Christmas Tree and I are a little freaked out about the horde coming our way."

"That's partly why we're reaching out to you Christmas Tree. What we know of your structure suggests you might survive. We have some advice for you to increase your chances."

"We're listening, Frank."

"First it is imperative you destroy the stairs to your deck. Preferably, you should take down the whole thing. I am looking at photos of your house right now; you cannot risk a horde pressing against a sliding glass door. Can you do that Christmas Tree?"

"That's been worrying us too Frank. We'll find a way." Photos of our house?

"Second, it is important that you brace your garage door. It faces the direction of the horde's march. The door has sufficient surface area to permit enough Zeke's to press against it potentially causing it to fail."

I thought about how to do this for a moment but came up with nothing. Ruth Ann shrugged as well when I shook my head at her.

"We don't know how we'll do that Frank."

"If you have a vehicle inside the garage, back it up against the inside of the door and engage the parking brake. This will provide support."

"That's a good idea. It sounds like this has come up before."

"It has Christmas Tree. You say you found a survivor, the son of your neighbors to the northwest? Would that be the house whose roof our folks saw you on the other day?"

"Yes."

"That's good to hear. We'll make a note. Say, there is something you can do for us Christmas Tree. You have enough IR to be lit up like, well, a Christmas tree, hence your call sign. We assume you have cameras?"

"Yes, Frank we have eight."

"Good. There is a network port on the radio. We want you to jack us into your cameras. I'm told the procedure is simple for a person with your background. The manual contains the information you'll need."

"I'll check it out. Say Frank? Don't you want to call me Walter?"

We heard a chuckle.

"OK Walter, you know you're the first person to pick up on that."

I looked up at Ruth Ann and told her that if I can be Cary Grant, she must be Leslie Caron.

"Walter, use preset 2 only for emergencies. If you need to contact me for more routine business, use present 1, OK?"

"OK, Frank. I'll probably call you if I get the cameras connected to confirm you are receiving. Say, are you really at Lambeau Field? The radio updates haven't said anything about troops reaching that far."

"Someday soon, Walter. Someday soon. Lambeau Field out."

Ruth Ann turned to me and said, "It'll be a sweet day when there are cheese heads back in Lambeau."

"I bet you and I have moved up a lot on the season ticket waiting list. Rough way to do it. Wouldn't it be great if the first game we played was against the Bears?"

"That would be great. I bet *you* I know the first thing that every true Packer fan will think when it happens," Ruth Ann's native Wisconsin background was showing.

"What's that?"

"After further review, the Bears still suck."

◆ We ate our dinner. Then I read the appropriate sections of the radio manual. It would be straightforward to give Frank a feed of still pictures from our security cameras. Best of all, the entire radio is digital so I could send data and still use the device as a radio at the same time.

I hooked up the Ethernet port to the house network and saw it pick up an IP address automatically as I expected. All I had to do was write some scripts to grab stills from the DVR's own web server and *scp* them to the radio. A mode on the radio told it to transmit then delete any file copied to it. I didn't have to worry about how to send it or where, that was all pre-programmed in the radio.

I cobbled together the scripts and verified with Lambeau Field that they were getting two 640 x 400 JPEG images per second. In total each camera sent one picture every four seconds.

Writing scripts was a welcome diversion. For me it was a brief return to "normal."

Later we went to the roof for a few minutes of chores before dark. I dusted the solar panels to rid them of the dirt kicked up by the Blackhawk. Ruth Ann policed the area collecting spent cartridges and other assorted crap. The greenhouse was closed up tight to conserve heat rising from an opened duct leading up from the basement, a poor man's geothermal heating.

We went back downstairs. I checked on Ryan. He said he was "fine." I told him he might hear some noise from a military operation that was expected to begin at any time.

Today's update broadcast said the next Twin Cities thinning operation would be this evening. We figured the horde had reached the Red Cedar River by now and was beginning to bunch up.

Ruth Ann and I went back to the roof to see what we could. The commencement of the thinning operation announced itself with distinct sounds of explosions. Unlike the previous night, these could be readily seen and heard. There were definitely closer.

As a horde comes against a natural obstacle such as Lake Menomin and the Red Cedar River it starts to bunch up before ultimately finding a way over or around.

Killing the dead is way more difficult than killing the living. Except to help increase the rate of decay (a long-term benefit), an otherwise traumatic injury is as good as a miss. Blowing an arm off or creating a gaping hole in a zombie's chest doesn't even slow him down. Destroying the brain stem is the only means of putting it down for good. To kill creatures in large numbers you have to pack them together to get a bigger bang from your bomb.

As soon as it was concluded that the creatures rotted over time, the "National Command Authority" determined to limit the destruction of strategic infrastructure where possible. If the dead could be reduced in numbers, thinned, so as not to pose an imminent risk to refugee centers the armed forces used a strategy of defense-in-depth.

There would be no nukes on American soil like in some of the pre-war fiction books I had read. Major bridges and the like would be spared unless absolutely necessary. In fact, major bridges were useful in keeping hordes bunched up longer. Bridges acted as escape valves keeping the horde on the other side moving forward *slowly* instead of fanning out. Without the escape valve to funnel a horde in a predictable direction, there would be no guarantee of keeping it together.

The sounds and glows of explosions and fires were most intense in the direction of Menominee. We were certain the buildings on the western bank of the unfrozen Red Cedar River were ablaze. Over the next few hours explosions and fires ranged further and further to the north and south of Interstate 94. We thought we heard a steady drone of jet engines that was quite different from the sound of fighters we had seen at airshows.

These sounded more like jumbo jets. Judging from an enormous spike in explosions and flames, large amounts of explosives were being dropped west of Menominee WI.

A bridge like the one on Hudson Road might be sacrificed to keep the horde bunched up longer but the main highway's bridge would be left standing. Eventually the horde would cross but not without being confined as long as possible where bombs and missiles could do the most good.

Nothing could be left alive out there. Unfortunately, leaving nothing alive was no longer sufficient.

The pounding went on for hours. Ruth Ann and I stayed on the roof until we were too cold. The wind really picked up and carried with it the smell of burning wood and a strong scent of something that was repulsive.

We made sure the house was shut down to its lowest level of functioning with the new addition of the tactical radio. We checked on Ryan once more and wished him a good night. He was holding up "fine." His voice conveyed no hint of sickness.

It was chilly upstairs at night though with plenty of blankets and covers we could still make do if we wanted to. We felt a lot more comfortable upstairs even with the windows blacked out than our first floor or basement. With a big day tomorrow though, we decided to sleep in the basement where it was warmer and no sound or vibration could reach us.

◆ After we rose Monday morning (Day 33), we discussed what we needed to get done for the day. A horde of nearly two million undead was to pass through our area by late afternoon. The horde would cover a big area so we had no way of knowing what the density of the dead would be at our location. From the radio updates and the warnings Frank gave us the day before, the density would be high enough that just pushing and shoving could threaten the integrity of our garage door and the heavy-duty super-duper premium patio door.

"Too bad we don't have a chainsaw," I said over a hot cup of tea.

"Why, do you want to go all "Doom" on the zombies?"

"As fun as that may sound," I said sarcastically, "we could really use one to take down the deck."

"Are you sure you don't want to take down just the stairs?"

"We don't really have the tools. I think it will actually be easier to tear the whole thing down taking the stairs down with it."

"Frank did say it would be better to get rid of the whole thing. He sounded like he knows what he's talking about." Ruth Ann said.

"Plus, getting rid of the deck gives us better views on cameras one and two. The problem remains, how do we get it down?"

"Ryan has a 4x4. Maybe it has a winch."

"If he doesn't have a winch that kind of car usually has a towing hitch or heavy duty bumpers. We have rope we can tie around the legs of the deck and drag them out from underneath." This seemed like a good solution.

We talked about letting Ryan out of the garage early. We wanted him to stay in there for a full 24 hours, which would be early afternoon. However, we needed his help now.

I looked directly into Ruth Ann's eyes and asked, "If he looks sick at all, if he's sweating or has puffy eyes, a runny nose, anything; we agree we'll kill him right?"

She looked at me. Then she looked through me.

"Ruth Ann? We can't take a chance. If he's sick we kill him where he stands. OK?"

"And by "we" you mean me again, right?"

I nodded.

◆ We didn't have to rouse Ryan from slumber. He sounded awake and alert which made us hopeful we would not go near the decision we had just made. Ruth Ann held the carbine in a ready position.

"Ryan, we have some TP for you. Stand away from the door and we'll toss it in." We discussed not telling Ryan we were checking him out to determine whether he lived or died. Some things are best left unsaid. In truth, I wasn't even holding toilet paper. I was holding the snub-nosed revolver.

"Tell us when you're on the other side of the garage."

"I'm fine. What's the big deal?"

"There's no big deal. We are just being careful for ourselves, OK. You can understand that, right?"

"Yeah, it's OK. This was way nicer than what they do in the camps."

We heard movement in the garage away from the door. His voice sounded more distant when he said "Fine. I'm ready." One more "fine" out of him I'd have shot Ryan if he was sick or not.

I unbolted the door, carefully listening for movement while I did so. I turned to Ruth Ann and she nodded. I opened the door. Ryan was near the garage door across the room from us. He was in the clean clothes we had put out for him but obviously needed some soap and a sponge bath. His color was normal. No sweating, no redness in his eyes, no sign of sickness.

I turned to Ruth Ann who was hidden from Ryan's view, nodded, and said it was OK. Ruth Ann stepped to the doorway keeping the carbine obscured by the wall.

"Actually Ryan," she said. "We have decided to end your "quarantine" a little early. We have been in touch with the authorities in Door County. A Blackhawk landed right outside, you probably heard it. They gave us a radio. There are almost two million zombies due to walk through here this afternoon. We could use your help to get ready."

Ryan's eyes got big when he heard that. I was still on guard – as his eyes got big, they were clear and sharp.

"Did you talk to them about me?"

"We told them a neighbor's son was here. It sounded like they didn't want to use names. They said they'd make a note of you being here."

I wondered if he was expressing concern for the horde or that we had talked to Lambeau Field about him. We still didn't know why he left there.

"Oh, OK – that's great. Can I have some real breakfast? I'm kind of tired of energy bars."

"Sure. Come on. Do you like tea?" I said as we moved to let the first person other than Ruth Ann and me into our fortress in more than a month.

"I'd rather have coffee."

Damn. Less for me.

◆ While Ryan ate we explained what we had learned from Frank and the radio update the night before. We checked the cameras and made our plan.

Ruth Ann would man the roof as top cover with the long range of her hunting rifle. I'd drive Ryan's 4x4 while he connected ropes to the legs of our deck.

"We should unbolt the joists," Ryan said.

"The what?"

"The deck is probably bolted to the house. We should remove the bolts first before we try pulling the deck down. If we don't, pulling the legs out will just collapse the deck. It won't pull it away. Do you have a socket set?"

I turned blankly to Ruth Ann. She was keeper of the tools in this house.

"Yes, we have a set," she said.

"Yes, we have a set," I repeated so as to maintain the appearance that I knew what I was doing.

"Maybe you should remove the bolts as the first step. It won't make much noise. Who knows what you'll attract when you drive Ryan's car over," Ruth Ann added.

When we were ready to start, Ryan and I opened the deck door and peered down between the slats to ensure nothing was waiting for us like under Flynn's deck. With Ruth Ann providing cover and keeping watch of the cameras on a tablet, Ryan and I loosened the heavy bolts. Even helping just this first time, saving Ryan proved worthwhile. I could not have undone the bolts by myself. The deck wobbled not being attached to the house. Bringing it down would be easy.

I grabbed the carbine (Ruth Ann felt comfortable that I was no longer a danger to myself or her). She confirmed the path to Ryan's 4x4 was clear as far as she could see. I handed Ryan the revolver for his own defense. He confirmed the weapon's load, something I still would not have thought of doing myself. I was getting the sense that the kid had more smarts about surviving outside the protection of a bunker like ours than either Ruth Ann or me.

He and I loped out to the southwest side of his parent's garage. He readied his car keys and the revolver. He turned the corner to the front of his house with the revolver raised. Even before taking a step he fired twice. I stepped around and saw that he had dispatched two rotting undead.

"This is the fuck that saw me go up the ladder and started all the banging," he whispered. He pointed the revolver at the smaller of the cadavers. It had bloody rotten nubs instead of hands. Whether it lost its hands when it was initially infected or wore them down banging and clawing to get Ryan and who knows who else before that we will never know.

I stepped back to where Ruth Ann could see us and signed her thumbs up to let her know we were OK. We saw that the report of Ryan's shots perked up a half dozen undead beyond the Boetche's house and an equal number beyond my house. We would be driving away from the first group but towards the second. As I got into the car with Ryan I heard Ruth Ann's hunting rifle begin a one sided conversation.

We arrived at our deck. Ryan vacated the driver's seat taking the rope we had left at the base of the deck's stairs. I got into the driver's seat. I caught myself reaching to adjust the mirrors. I laughed.

While Ryan wound rope around both of the outer deck legs and made the loops fast with some kind of knot, I backed Ryan's car up to be in line with the centerline of the deck. Ryan attached the rope to his trailer hitch and tapped the side of the car twice. I put the car in low gear and took up the slack slowly.

The deck came away from the house easily. Ruth Ann shouted that a creature was coming around the south side of our house, along the path we had just driven. Ryan readied his revolver as the ghoul appeared. By its clothing, it was a former firefighter. Ryan dispatched him easily. After we were done with the deck I read his shoulder patch and was sad to see he was from our own local department. Would I have been less sad if it were from someone else's town?

Ruth Ann continued to take out approaching zombies. Her rate of fire began to ratchet upwards. I knew she would be taking careful aim and pacing herself. The increased rate of fire did not bode well. I continued to drag the deck, which had now collapsed, away from the house. Ryan walked along side. He reached into the car and extracted my carbine. He raised it to his shoulder and fired across the car parallel to the windshield. The kid was good with weapons and executed the undead woman with easy grace. He placed the weapon back in the car then unhooked the rope from the trailer hitch. He jumped in and I drove us the short distance to the front of my garage.

I had thought about positioning the collapsing deck over the water well's head. I was very worried about damage to the water pump. I decided not to use the collapsed deck as a shield for the pump housing as the oncoming dead might force the deck against the wellhead doing even more damage. Besides, I had a different idea about how to protect the wellhead.

Before going outside I had detached the garage door from its lift chain and undid its hasps. Ryan hopped out of the car and easily rolled the door upwards. I pulled his 4x4 into our garage alongside our station wagon. He stepped inside the garage and let the door down. We left the door unhitched from its lift chain and slid the door's hasps into place making it impossible to lift under power or manually.

With hand signals he helped me back his car up to the left half of the garage door. I made soft contact with the door and then gave it just a little more pressure. I shut off the 4x4, engaged the parking break then we repeated the same process with my car.

Both of our must-do jobs were done. Ryan and I joined Ruth Ann on the roof. I got some more practice with the carbine and Ryan demonstrated he needed no practice with the hunting rifle.

We weren't supposed to worry about our front and back doors. The ghouls wouldn't actively be trying to break down these doors if they didn't know we were inside. Frank told us the dead would not be able to bring enough bodies to bear on a surface as small as a single door without being motivated.

Still, the front door at least continued to worry me. If the creatures succeeded in breaking down the back door they would enter the garage. They would have to break down another heavy door to gain access to us. If they got through the front door on the other hand, we'd instantly lose two floors of the house. We would be either trapped on the roof or trapped in the basement.

I fetched a fancy webcam out of an office drawer. It was designed to be a baby monitor so it had sound and two rings of IR LEDs for night vision built in. I ran an extension cord from a hot socket to near the front door. I powered up the webcam and placed it on the floor with a view of the front entryway. A few moments later we had an HD view of the inside of the front door.

In the garage, Ryan helped me rig an ordinary cheapo USB webcam up to a Raspberry Pi. We positioned this to give us a view of anything coming towards the inner door. I wished the neighbor who thought I was nuts for putting RJ45 network jacks in my garage was here to see me make use of them. Sure, it took a zombie apocalypse to need it, but still...

After we were done Ruth Ann asked "Doug, what's the point of a camera watching the front door? It's not going to slow them down if they make it in."

"They're not supposed to be motivated enough to try to bust the door down. But if they do, we'll have some advance warning." In reality, I was only trying to keep busy to hide my nervousness about the oncoming horde.

Ruth Ann put me in my place with her reply, “You’ll have really great shots of them coming in if you’re wrong.”

◆ We made other needed preparations around the house, working until noon. I switched on the AM radio for the day's update. We listened together as we ate lunch. The thinning operation had gone well.

They estimated ten percent of the Twin Cities horde had been put down or so severely maimed as to be immobile. It was difficult for me to comprehend that conventional weapons killed 200,000 formerly human beings in one night.

In my imagination I could see so many bodies pressed into the Red Cedar River as to actually block it. The dead coming up from behind wouldn't need the I-94 Bridge – they could walk over the bodies of their comrades. Later, I asked Frank about this and he said only "Yeah, that's about right."

The mega-horde, Chicago B, was near Janesville Wisconsin. If it turned north, it was possible that Madison, the Berkeley of the Midwest and ground zero of this whole catastrophe would suffer the additional ignominy of being trampled under the weight of four million FIPs.

After passing through us, the Twin Cities horde would be hammered by the military along the Chippewa River just as Chicago B would be hit along the Rock River.

It struck me how much the dead's behavior was that of a flock of birds or herd of beasts. I wondered if they could be steered. We learned that analysts used the same observation and asked the same question. They developed techniques giving a limited ability to steer or even split hordes and we would play a part in it.

There was no opportunity to steer the Twin Cities horde now though. They were too close and there was not a terrain feature between them and us that could be used as a wedge. We'd be in the middle of the TC horde shortly.

The dead wandering around our development already appeared to be agitated. At first we thought they'd converge on our house due to the noise we were just making. After watching the cameras for a few minutes it became clear we were not the dead's focus. Could they somehow know that the horde was coming? Probably not because we soon saw a wave of wildlife hustling through our neighborhood heading away from approaching horde. The deer, turkeys and other assorted critters that were racing eastward, excited the dead.

◆ Around three thirty, the three of us bundled up and went up to the roof to watch for the arrival of the Twin Cities horde. We kept low over the wall or out of sight completely using the drainage ports in the parapet walls. As we looked west signs of the horde were immediately apparent.

Less than a mile west, beyond 20th street, the woods surrounding the little Elk Creek seemed to shake. Elk Creek wasn't wide, deep or swift enough to present an obstacle to the horde. It might even have been frozen over, I wasn't about to check.

Dark figures emerged from the tree line. We could not see I-94 to our south from our roof but we could see the smaller and closer US-12. It was boiling with shapes.

The first ghouls through the woods were in sorry shape, even for undead. Through our binoculars I saw tattered burnt clothing on badly disfigured and charred bodies. Even as far away as they were the noise they made was terrible to hear. It was a nonstop drone of low frequency growls punctuated by higher frequency unintelligible screaming. Blind pure unthinking rage filtered across the distance between us.

As the slow moving train wreck came closer I could discern many faces completely denuded of skin. I saw ghastly skulls with bared eyeballs and teeth. Some had remnants of arms hanging uselessly at their sides. All showed evidence of burns that would have felled any living human. These ghouls had literally walked through fire and come out the other side but I doubted they would appear on any self-help infomercials anytime soon.

A seemingly endless stream of dead left the tree line heading towards us. The open space dwindled moment by moment. We were held transfixed. Like people on a beach hoping the incoming tide would change its mind and turn around, we were helpless.

The leading edge of the horde disappeared behind the trees lining 20th Street. Soon after, the trees began to shake. We saw younger trees go down as the leading edge plowed over the berm and down into our own neighborhood beyond the Boetche's house.

From in front of the unstoppable wave fast motion caught our attention. A figure ran hard towards Flynn's. The quickly moving figure could not be one the dead. He moved far too fast and too "naturally" be to one of them. In a flash, he disappeared behind what would be to him the front of Flynn's house. He must have gained entry because he did not come out the back.

Suddenly, from the very sliding door we had used to make our own entry, glass shattered and fell. The man, already bloody, got one foot onto the deck before arms, too many to count, grabbed at the man and pulled him back into the house. We could not hear the man's last screams over the noise of the horde. The dead were streaming past the Boetche's and exploded out of the back of the Flynn's. So many dead flowed onto the Flynn's deck that they knocked themselves over the railings and down the steps. In a crash, the Flynn's deck failed completely. Dead continued to stream out of the hole that had been the sliding door only to drop on their fellows below.

The sound was deafening now. The horde was *here*. At the foot of *my* house. In a moment, we were surrounded. I had a memory of some Western I had seen as a child where a cowboy and his leading lady were surrounded by a stampede of cattle. The cowboy in his impossibly white hat calmly turned to his woman and told her not to be afraid. Ruth Ann and I now sat knees to our chests with our backs to the parapet wall. I turned to her and was more afraid than at any time in my life. I couldn't tell her not to be afraid. I couldn't get a sound to come out.

It was time to go inside.

◆ We crept down from the roof level to our second story. The reinforced concrete walls shook. The second floor's windows backed by blankets did nothing to lessen the skull-splitting din from outside. Ryan made his way towards a front-facing window. Ruth Ann stopped him.

"I want to see them," Ryan shouted.

"We can see them well enough on the cameras," she replied and pulled him away from the windows.

Actually, we could see them too well on the cameras. They were up high but had a direct view. With no intervening wall to give the impression of separation, the camera views were even more visceral than being on the roof. Seeing all eight views at once made it brutally clear how surrounded we truly were. As far as the cameras could see we were in a crush of grinding death.

There was a steady current of dead impacting our front and garage doors. From downstairs came the sound of thudding against the front door synchronized with the images we watched on screen. I was comforted by the thuds as they weren't purposeful pounding. Sometimes a particularly loud bang travelled up the stairs but we could see that this corresponded to a knee or head that bounced backwards and staggered on.

I had hoped that the density of the dead would actually work for us, and it was. Individuals didn't have much time to become aroused by something particular about the house before they were bumped and shoved from behind by more dead. As long as we remained hidden and the doors held, we would probably survive.

However, I did have a significant and justified concern for our water well. If we were to lose our pump, we would be without water and therefore in an indefensible fortress. No refuge no matter how secure can provide safety for more than a few days without water. A house call from the plumbers would likely be a very long wait.

The well rose above ground in a small knee-high structure about 15 yards from the house. The dead were banging into the wellhead even now. As bad as it was outside, we had to go back upstairs to implement my plan to protect the well enclosure.

"We can't risk damage to the well," I said to mutual agreement. "I want to make an obstacle in front of the well that will cause them to flow around it."

"What are you going to use to do that?" said Ruth Ann.

"Them. He wants to use them," Ryan caught on immediately. Ruth Ann looked confused.

"I want to drop some of them with the bow just "upstream" of the well. I think if we can drop enough of them in the right spot, the rest will just flow around."

"Even if they climb over the well it would be better than constantly kicking it. Enough kicking and that thing will come apart," said Ryan. "I could use the crossbow. I always wanted to use a crossbow."

In the few hours he'd been out of the garage Ryan alternately annoyed, puzzled, scared and impressed me. This was all in a day's Xbox for him.

Ruth Ann agreed with the concept but expressed concern about drawing attention to ourselves and our sanctuary.

Safeguarding our water supply was worth the risk. "They won't be able to process why the zombie in front of them suddenly fell over. Let's try some shots and see what happens. If we draw any attention we'll figure out something else."

I had no "something else." It was either this plan or nothing.

We had about two hours of daylight left. I considered passing out foam earplugs but figured it would only make it harder for us to hear each other while doing little about the sound of the horde. The sound of the horde permeated our bodies. We would hear it no matter what we stuck in our ears. I handed Ryan a dozen crossbow bolts and the crossbow making his day. Ruth Ann took as many arrows as she should carry along with her recurve bow. I took a freshly charged laptop with which to monitor the cameras.

As bad as the noise was the affront to our ears was nothing compared to the insult hurled against our noses. Mixed with an overwhelming rotting smell was the odor of charred flesh. The stench was unbearable.

We crept low to the northeastward facing wall. I had drawn pictures downstairs of how I hoped to layout bodies in an arc around and over the wellhead.

Ruth Ann and Ryan loaded their weapons. They would fire our first salvo together and then drop down behind the shelter of the parapet wall. Each of us exchanged a nod with the others. Both shooters got up only as high as needed to clear the wall, aimed and fired. Even standing next to them, I heard nothing from either weapon.

Nevertheless I tugged on both their jackets. We would watch the results on camera and not risk any more time above the wall than necessary. It was impossible to tell what the missiles had hit. There was a disturbance in the flow near the wellhead with creatures falling over each other.

There was no reaction that would indicate they were aware that they had been attacked or where the attack had come from. Ruth Ann and Ryan repeated the process again, taking a little more time to aim. This time I saw the missiles reach their terminus in the skulls of two walkers. They went down immediately adding to the turbulence near the wellhead.

A few yards behind some heads were turning up and to their right towards the origin of the streaks they must have seen. Seeing nothing some returned their gaze to what passed for straight ahead depending upon their disfigurement. A few continued looking in our direction. In a stroke of good fortune, the ghouls who lingered looking up at us tripped right over the creatures we had just shot.

Shoot, hide, observe.

We repeated this over and over again until a mound of three dozen bodies protected the wellhead. The dead flowed around and over the mound like water around a big rock.

We got off the roof as soon as our task was done.

◆ The noise was driving us nuts. We could choose to not look at the cameras but we could not avoid the noise while on the second floor. We collected our weapons, some tech and blankets and headed to the first floor. On the way past the kitchen table I checked on the tactical radio, it was still transmitting.

The solid walls of the first floor vibrated just as much as those of the second. The small non-operating strip windows kept out more of the sound. With earplugs, it might have been almost livable on this level. The immediacy of the thudding against the front door, though, made staying on the first floor impossible. Every bang or scrap against the front door reminded me, at least, how little a separation there was between the horde outside and the three of us in here.

We would be heading to the basement in a moment but I wanted to look for myself to see how well the front door was holding up. I crept to the door imagining that at any moment it would burst inwards. It was just getting dark outside and I could see nothing through the blacked out sidelights. A hand must have slapped the beveled glass. It was then that truly I appreciated how fragile the sidelights were. The looters had used a baseball bat on our neighbors' houses. Continued knees and slaps would be just as effective here over time. What about a creature with just the right slap wearing just the right jewelry?

I checked the deadbolt and hasp on the floor. The upper hasp was locked from visual inspection as I couldn't bring myself to stand up to check it. I could feel every bang against the door. The sound of their moaning just inches from my head made my skin crawl. What I checked looked good. The baby monitor webcam was in place so I got the hell away from there.

We headed through the door leading to the basement.

We turned on some hand cranked LED camp lights on their lowest settings and continued on into the basement. Ruth Ann was the last one down and dead bolted the door behind us. At least this door didn't have any fucking sidelights.

The good news was that it was quiet. Virtually no sound reached us through the foundation. The bad news is that should any entry be made into the house we would be trapped. But who was I kidding? Millions of cold dead eating machines were walking through our yard. If they got in the house whether we were here or upstairs we'd soon be one of them.

Cranking up a few more camp lights we started making ourselves comfortable. We had no cooking equipment set up down here yet but we could set up an electric hot plate if we needed one (and electricity held out). There were plenty of non-perishables and dry goods. This is also where we kept our canned goods. If we were trapped down here, as long as we could replenish water we could last a long time. Deep down I knew the basement door would give out long before the food did.

For the next few hours it might have passed for a sleepover except that the zombie movie we watched was a live video feed.

While I was down here I figured I might as well do some tidying up while Ruth Ann and Ryan talked. I could hear Ruth Ann edging around the question we were wanting an answer to since we first discovered Ryan. Again, he steered the conversation away from the subject. I resolved that in the morning, if morning came, I would ask the question directly and insist upon an answer.

It didn't take me long to check in on our batteries and power status, all good. I nosed through our long term supplies, all good there too. I scored a bonus when I ran across a small sample box of cups for the coffee machine upstairs. The box had long ago expired and many of the flavors were crap but there were a couple of good ones in there. I would just need access to a machine two floors up.

Finally, I looked in longingly on my technological pride and joys sitting idle since the shit hit the fan. The work I did in

Silicon Valley required lots of processing power and tons of storage. When I “retired” to Wisconsin I saw no reason to be without the toys to which I had become accustomed. I had a few ideas I was working on. I could have rented “cloud” services for processing power but this was not just my work. Fiddling with wires and buttons was my hobby as well. Ruth Ann had her greenhouse; I had my own farm of sorts.

As such farms went it wasn’t large but for things one might find in a residential basement, it was huge. Two 12U racks each sported a dozen servers. Each server was capable of running tens of web sites each fairly well. Hundreds each, badly. The servers were fed by two 18 terabyte networked attached storage (NAS) arrays. Next to those was my own small supercomputer. The box held four Tesla K10s that together were many thousands of very fast computer cores perfect for image processing and parallel computing.

While I could occasionally fire up one the NAS devices for fetching this or that such as a ripped movie or book, the servers were a power impossibility. There was enough horsepower and storage sitting idle here to run hundreds of web servers. Even if I had the power to run them I would still be missing the web itself. Still, they looked pretty and I patted the boxes lovingly.

I came back to the big room and stretched out on the couch with a few layers on blankets on top. I flipped on my tablet. When it connected to the house, the status indicator for email showed up. I had been with Ruth Ann and Ryan all day. They hadn’t sent me anything. I opened up the email app and found the message was from our modem / router. A modem, or modulator / demodulator, is the thing that physically connects the network inside the house (the LAN) to the outside world (the WAN). The modem was on whether we had Internet service or not as it was also the device that told packets inside the house how to get from one device to another (routing). The modem had sent me an email saying that for about a minute early this morning, it had a connection to the outside world! For a minute, we had Internet service!

While this was very exciting, I didn't share the news as I had no idea what it meant.

◆ We watched the steady crush of dead lessen slowly to a consistent but lighter flow past our house. The percentage of badly burned creatures had dropped to almost zero.

I suppose we can all take pride in the diversity of the dead. A butcher, a baker and probably a candlestick maker had undoubtedly passed our cameras amidst the slowly advancing horde. Every race, color and from what we could tell by jewelry and apparel most creeds were represented. We are all clearly equal in the end.

Just watch the time-lapse stills from our cameras that DHS put up at the War Memorial website. It turns out our house's camera feed was the first ground level "live and in-the-round" look at the inside of a horde of undead.

We had been watching a long time now. The density of the dead had come down to the point where we could once again concentrate on individuals. Ruth Ann stopped watching completely after a woman passed right under camera five wearing a wrap style baby carrier. That's the type where the infant faces mom or dad, arms and legs poking out like a starfish. The woman and child were truly heartbreaking as the infant's arms and legs were where they were supposed to be but there was no head on the child. Instead, the remains of a spine poked up from the bloody baby sling. The woman's face, hands and arms were stained with the dried blood of her own baby. You can see the mother and child about two hours and twenty-one minutes into the time-lapse video. You can see it if you want to. We've tried desperately to forget it.

I asked Ryan what he meant about staying overnight in our garage being better than what they do at the camps.

"If you come in by car, soldiers guide you inside a big garage. You drive up to really tight lanes made from those temporary concrete guardrails from when they do road work, you know? There isn't enough room to open your doors. They tell you to put your car in neutral, roll up all your windows except for the driver's. That one stays open enough to pass water bottles and food in. They give you enough water and protein bars to last 24 hours. From there on in, if you start your car they'll shoot you right through the window."

Wow. Martial law really means martial law.

"They push you down the lane until you bump the car ahead of you. You stay like that for 24 hours. If anyone turns inside your car, you'll all be dead. If the zombie doesn't kill you they don't take any chances. They shoot everyone in the car anyway."

This made perfect sense and must be very effective.

"What if you don't come with a car?" Ruth Ann asked.

"They zip cord your feet together and stuff you in a sleeping bag. Then they zip cord your hands and close up the bag. They put a straw next to your face for water. No protein bars. Then you wait 24 hours. If you have to pee, you pee. If you have to crap, you crap. It is way less comfortable than being in a car. At least you can move around in a car. But then again, you won't get eaten by a family member if they turn. That happened a lot," Ryan was looking downwards as he talked.

"So after 24 hours they look you over. If you look sick it's a .45 to the head. If a family member looks sick, it's a .45 to the head. If you've turned, it's a .45 to the head. Simple. And no chance to spread the infection." Ryan made the motion of shooting a pistol into the side of his head.

"If you make it through, you spray down and wash you up. They give you new clothes. That's pretty much it. Once in a camp there's hardly ever an infection. They do this to every person coming in. Even soldiers coming in from patrol. If you refuse, it's a .45 to the head. Sort of like "Is that your final answer?" Bang!" he finished.

Later with Ryan out of earshot, Ruth Ann and I discussed his story of camp life.

"Do you think he's exaggerating at all?" I said.

"Definitely, he's got it wrong."

“Really? What part?”

“The .45 hasn’t been standard issue for years.”

When the cameras switched from daylight color to infrared black and white I realized how long we had been transfixed by the scene outside. I did not want leave the quiet of the basement but I wanted to let Lambeau Field know we were doing OK. The radio, however, remained on the second floor.

I typed up a message and saved it to a file called ‘readme.txt”. In it, I gave Frank an update saying we were safe in the basement for reasons of maintaining sanity. We would check in by voice when the horde had passed. I copied the readme file to the radio and sure enough within seconds, it disappeared, deleted by the radio itself after transmission.

◆ I was dozing off and Ruth Ann was sewing when Ryan shouted for us to come to the laptop. The all-camera view was up. Ryan pointed at camera six, which showed a view along the front of the house looking northeast. Where the front door would be I could see a spastically waving arm connected to an immobile shoulder. Part of an upper torso seemed to stick out of the wall. I instantly knew what had happened. Murphy, you mother fucker.

I hit a key to fill the screen with camera six. A monster was wedged partially through one of the sidelights at the front door. Its head was through the opening along with its left arm. It was wedged at its chest. Perhaps it hung up on its clothes or maybe by the size of his body. I could not tell.

I pulled the laptop to me and opened the baby monitor's built-in web server. In pristine infrared HD we looked directly at a shoulder and wildly waving downward pointed arm. There were jagged glass pieces on the floor. It fingers and jaw snapped open and closed. It could almost rake jagged fingernails across the smooth tile floor. What we could see of its head was covered with matted blood-caked hair as it continuously flailed about. After a moment, we could clearly see the thing had sliced or torn its own ears off possibly when getting through the opening. It snarled and snapped at the air around it.

For a moment I enabled the monitor's audio, our end muted. The sound of a horde is terrible. The sound of just one monster only a few feet away is even more terrifying. I muted the audio immediately.

Its head was clearly through the opening. It was bashing its left arm against the inside of the door itself and against the wood trim below the broken sidelight. We still could not tell if it was hung up on clothes that could suddenly tear loose. Or, was it unable to get its torso through? One alternative meant some security while the other meant none. We had to act.

"I am loading the crossbow!" Ruth Ann said.

“Are you going up there?” I said.

“We have to kill that thing before it gets in. Where it is we can use its body to plug up the break. We have to do it now!”

“And by “we” you mean you again, right?”

She looked at me. “How many crossbows have you fired, Doug?” Ruth Ann got the crossbow, cocked it and made sure the safety was on. Then she snapped a stubby evil looking bolt in place. She picked up the revolver and put it in her pocket. “Don’t worry,” she said. “Easier than shooting fish in a barrel.”

I grabbed the carbine. With Ryan carrying the laptop so we could watch the baby monitor, all three of us made our way up the stairs to the bolted door. We clicked the one camp light we brought off and waited in total darkness for our pupils to dilate. We checked the baby monitor. The beast was still wedged in the sidelight. Ruth Ann unbolted the door leading out of the basement. There was no mute button now.

I moved out first so I could ready myself behind Ruth Ann as backup. Ruth Ann settled into a crouch with the cross bow at the ready. Ryan watched the laptop. His face glowed faintly. There was minimally enough light for us to see. Ryan nodded at Ruth Ann and whispered, “He’s still stuck - no change.”

“OK. You ready hon?” she said softly. I love it when my wife uses endearments before we shoot a snarling ghoul. Actually, this was the first time this situation had come up.

“Yeah.”

“OK, on three.” She stood up just behind the wall turning into our entryway. The crossbow was up and ready. She counted to three. Ruth Ann pivoted around the corner. The beast looked up and roared. The crossbow answered.

The beast fell silent instantly.

Ruth Ann pivoted back towards the open basement door. Ryan scurried down using the laptop screen for light, followed by Ruth Ann. I bolted the door behind us.

At the base of the stairs, Ruth Ann and Ryan stared at the laptop. When I could see the screen too, I saw the creature's arm drooped and motionless, its head folded over its shoulder. Only a tiny nub of the missile's tail protruded from its skull. I flipped to outside camera six. We could see the now really dead undead thing poking out from the doorway just as limp on the outside (of the house) as it was on the inside.

"Doug?" said Ryan. "What's up with those windows? They're easy to get into."

"I'd rather not talk about it right now."

To calm myself I went about making a copy of the H.264 video file containing the whole movie of the home invader. I transferred the copy over to the radio for transmission to Lambeau Field. They saw the set up; they might as well get to see the big finish.

For the next hour, we watched the cameras intently. We saw the ghouls bounce around the creature stuffing the hole in our house without processing the opportunity they had. We saw the remaining structure of the deck we had torn down completely disappear under a pile of human shaped spastic worker ants. Finally, we saw their density thin down to a relative trickle. On the all-camera view, we could see only a few dozen stragglers wandering around.

We felt safe enough to take turns sleeping two at a time.

◆ Ruth Ann nudged me awake on Tuesday (Day 34), what would have been Election Day. Down in the basement there was no way to judge time. A tablet said it was a little after seven in the morning. The all-camera view showed clouds mixed with sprinkles of undead. The land looked like it was trampled by a horde of zombies. Oh wait, it was.

There was no change on the baby monitor except the pristine HD infrared picture was now a pristine HD color picture. What a miserable mess. The webcam in the garage showed nothing had changed in there. No breaches of any kind.

We gathered much of our things and walked up the flight of steps to the first floor. We stopped to scan the cameras again and listened to the stillness on the other side of the door. Opening up, nothing looked different as long as we did not look to the front door. We quietly made our way to the second floor where comforts including the kitchen awaited. I had a date with some coffee.

Actually, coffee presented the first of what would prove to be a day of changing directions. While still only thinking about firing up the brewing machine I glanced at the tactical radio sitting on the kitchen table. I remembered we had new demands on our power and wondered if I could use the ready-made cups with an electric kettle instead. I tried. It does not work. I tossed the box of stale samples in the back of the pantry and settled for some of the instant coffee we found at the Flynn's now off-limits house.

Breakfast consisted of cold cereal with powdered milk. Homemade strawberry jam mixed in made it palatable. Objectively we were still living like kings compared to most of the planet but it did not feel that way.

None of us wanted to talk. For my part, I did not know enough about the coming day to have anything worth saying and I did not want to talk about the past. We did and saw things in the last 24 hours that took the desire for conversation right out of us. What I wanted desperately was to get out on the roof and see things with my own eyes.

We bundled up. It was in the high 20's. On opening the door, there were moans and screams here and there from the assorted detritus roaming around below. We were grateful not to hear the sound of a whole horde.

We heard jets and explosions. Looking east, we could see smoke rising from the direction of Eau Claire only about seven miles away. Through our binoculars, I could clearly see shapes over the city. We had slept through the heaviest of the bombardment. What we saw and heard now was the tail end. The horde would have moved beyond the Chippewa River by now.

Ruth Ann and I want to take a moment to digress. We want to acknowledge the Carson Park survivors. Both you and we lived through the experience of praying that a horde would pass through without tearing our limbs apart and eating our beating hearts. We however endured nothing compared to you folks who, in addition to the horde, hunkered down amidst bombs, missiles and the carnage that comes with them. We will see you at the reunions and for as long as we live, the first round will always be on Ruth Ann and me.

It was a good thing that the sanctuary at Chippewa Valley Regional was evacuated two weeks ago. There was no possibility anyone there would have survived.

◆ The clouds said snow. They get a somber gray pregnant look before the flakes begin to fall. I imagined the land would look almost normal when covered in white. Sound would be deadened a bit, especially during the snow itself. That could be a good thing, as the deadening would deaden the sound of the dead.

We walked the periphery of the roof, surveying both out to the horizon and the state of things immediately below us. I had not noticed before that some of the fake first floor window shutters were torn off the house and were nowhere to be found. Some of the trees we argued with the ARC about so long ago were gone completely while others were denuded sticks without leaf or needle. Who knows if the perennial flowers we fought over were still safe underground, oblivious to the changes taking place above?

From what we could see of the Flynn's house, not a single window or door on the three levels facing us remained intact. Drapes fluttered outside. Looking through our binoculars Ruth Ann said there were things moving upright inside. There was movement visible under the wreckage of their deck.

Everywhere we looked the tall prairie grasses that we loved to watch wave in the wind were beaten down. Everything was trampled.

A covering of virginal white would be welcome.

Looking at the home to our east that had been looted we saw what Frank had warned us about. If the Olson's ever returned they would find every portal to their home crushed and debris everywhere. The back door leading out of their garage was off its hinges. The garage door itself was in pieces. The picture window that had once provided them a lovely view of our backyard was smashed out completely. There was movement in their home.

In every direction sprinkled here and there, including at the base of our house, were dead walking around or standing still like statues. Not counting creatures inside buildings that we could not see, we estimated about 80 dead remained in our immediate area.

As to the Boetche's house, Ryan's home, we couldn't really tell anything. It looked intact from our direction suggesting the front side was not breached. If the front had been breached, the back would surely have been as blown out at the Flynn's place.

I am sure the kid was anxious to check out his house, having left a safe area to drive two hundred miles through the dead to get here.

◆ Speaking of which, my mind was stuck in neutral. With all the things I should have been thinking about I found myself ruminating about why Ryan Boetche was here at all.

The kid told us he had left Door County, the largest safest settlement in the Midwest, to drive over two hundred miles to a house he knew was empty. His traveling partner, now deceased, was "regular army?" Why was he here?

"Listen Ryan, we've danced around the question long enough. Why are you here? Why was a soldier with you?"

"You guys wouldn't understand."

"Don't give me that shit. We are living through a zombie apocalypse. There's a lot we'd understand."

"You and Mrs. Handsman, you and my parents were friends."

"Yeah. We were. We are. They are good people. Did you see them in Door County? They were heading for your cottage."

"They didn't make it to the cottage. I don't know where they are. They weren't who you thought they were. We weren't who people thought we were."

"What are you talking about? Your father is a day trader and your mother is a stay-at-home mom who volunteers in the community. What is there to know? What are trying to say? You are from Remulak? You're in the witness protection program? What?"

Ryan looked past me to Ruth Ann. I could see in his eyes that what he was about to say was a door slamming shut on the "normal" life of his past. He could be chased onto a rooftop by walking dead. He could nonchalantly drill them in the skull. Telling us why he was here was harder because we knew him and his family before all this.

He took a deep breath.

"Dad wasn't a day trader, Doug. We grew dope. We grew a lot of really good dope. We were dope dealers. Hell we weren't just dealers, we were *the* source of authentic organic craft grown Mendocino Mind Fuck outside of Mendocino itself."

Ryan's face was red and his eyes were tearing. It was clear he was profoundly embarrassed. This is a very upscale neighborhood. Some people who lived here were overt elitist snobs. Everyone who lived here was on the upper end of the local socioeconomic food chain. Ryan's family grew dope.

"Mrs. Handsman, you remember all the advice you gave Mom about growing herbs? Well she grew herb. The entire basement of our house," he said pointing at his home, "is irrigation and lights and pumps and valves and shrink wrap machines and the only computers Dad used were for managing our grow."

"Ryan, kid, look at me," I said. "We know. We have one of your plants in the greenhouse. Your dad gave it to us on the day they left."

Ryan was apparently stunned and relieved. It seemed like an appropriate time for a group hug so I grabbed the kid and motioned Ruth Ann to join us. It was a real Norman Rockwell moment if Norman Rockwell painted families hugging while surrounded by undead looking for live flesh to feed upon instead of warm fires and mistletoe.

The hug ended.

"You still haven't answered my question. Why are you here now? Why did a soldier come with you? Are you in trouble?"

"Actually, no. They sent me."

"Who sent you?"

"The military."

"The military sent you?"

"Yeah. There are almost 300,000 people in Door County without much to do and nowhere to go. It may be martial law but the military knows a stressed-out group of people that large is dangerous. Dope is free in Door County. They hand it out."

"What? Why?" I wasn't parsing this yet.

"How many armed revolutions can you think of that were started by stoners? They're more likely to giggle than storm a wall."

"How many people smoke?" Ruth Ann said.

"Like every day? Around 30,000. More do it occasionally. Mom had about 60 keys of sealed product in the house when they left. That will last about two days in the County. But that's not the main reason they sent me."

"Which is?"

"To see if the grow room is OK. If it is I have to contact Lambeau Field for pick-up of our equipment, log books and our seed stock."

"Lambeau Field? What do you know about Lambeau Field?" Ryan hadn't heard my conversation and I hadn't used the term in front of him.

"That radio you got? I think it's more for me than you guys."

I was fucking livid.

That drug kingpins lived right next door did not bother me. That getting access to pot seeds to grow better dope was the actual impetus for helping us really angered me off. I'm a smart guy. Ruth Ann and I are good people. We lived in a goddamned fortress and the only reason to reach out to us was for some fucking dope for a nation of stoners?

What about after they got their pot farm? What of us? Are we back to fending for ourselves? A bunch of seeds and log books are more important than us? Apparently so.

◆ The radio was on preset two: emergency. Ryan was not around. He had made his call for pickup right after our conversation then I shooed him away.

"Frank, you remember I told you our neighbor's kid was with us, right."

"Yes, Walter."

"And you know perfectly well who he is, right?"

"Yes, Walter."

"And you know what his family business is?"

"Yes, Walter."

"And you sent him?"

"Not personally but the individual you are referring to is on official business. So yes, Walter."

"You know what Frank?"

"Yes, Walter?"

"Stop calling me fucking Walter! This is a digital radio. I know it's encrypted. You know it's encrypted. Just stop with the stupid call sign shit already. Come on out here, pick up your boy, pick up your dope and leave us the fuck alone."

I heard myself sounding like a Fox news watching survivalist antigovernment tea bagger but I couldn't stop. Spit flew as I yelled into the mike and I'm sure the veins in my neck were popping out. Ruth Ann grabbed the mike out of my hand and gave me the most tender "shut the fuck up" eyes I'd seen from her in a long time.

"Frank," she said, "this is Miss Goody Two Shoes. Walter is going to have a time out until he can use his inside voice again."

"I understand. We will be out later today to make the pick-up. We owe you an explanation and there's a proposition we'd like to make. We want you to understand that we really are doing the best we can under awful circumstances."

"Walter is upset about us being considered secondary to a weed patch, Frank. We are both upset about that. More so, we want to know where we fit in after you get what you came for. If you have a proposition for us we're listening."

"Understood. Your local law enforcement was tipped off a number of months ago by the electric utility that there was something going on in your neighborhood. At the risk of upsetting Walter even more, the sheriff's office assumed it was you at first. UPS was constantly at your house and your electric bill is high. Also, frankly, Walter isn't from around here and your house is a fort with no windows, perfect for a large grow operation."

"They quickly realized it wasn't you when they found your neighbor's electric bills were even higher than yours."

I was frothing at the mouth. Ruth Ann had to swat my hands away from the mike "Go on Frank," she said.

"The sheriff's office was about to raid your neighbor's house when the situation we find ourselves in right now came up. Since then priorities have changed. What they would have gone to prison for two months ago is now a valuable tool in getting people through this. Safe havens have been compromised because of insurrection among the people they were supposed to protect. About ten percent of our population here frequently makes use of the substance. That amounts to thousands of people we don't have to worry about making trouble."

"What do you do when they get the munchies? Bite each other?" I shouted, but Ruth Ann didn't have the transmit button pressed. Ruth Ann swatted me again but with her eyes this time.

"What about us Frank? You needed us to shelter Ryan but we've done that now. What becomes of us?"

"We know what kind of work Walter did in California. The sheriff's office had already subpoenaed your online purchase records, so we know what you have in your house. Walter, I hope you're listening. We believe you have in your basement the largest *defendable* data center in the Midwest Administrative Zone. We need it. Moreover, we need your talents."

Silently I laughed at the irony of being only a few miles from one of the world's premier makers of supercomputers that the military had finished bombing the place just a few hours before.

Apparently, my basement represented a better option because of its outsized capability paired with a small hardened defendable shell. And they needed my talents? These people fucking used me and now I am going to fucking use them.

I motioned for Ruth Ann to give me the mike back. She made eyes to me asking if I was going to be a good boy or not. I nodded yes, back to her. She handed me the mike.

"Frank, Walter here. Whatever it is you need me to do you have to make it possible for us to do it here. That's not negotiable."

"Walter, you and Miss Goody Two Shoes will be a lot more comfortable here. Let us pack you up and bring you to Lambeau Field."

"What part of non-negotiable don't you understand? We're not going to risk living among three hundred thousand potential happy meals. You guys are zombie bait. We're staying right here. You want me and my rigs, you make it happen."

Then a thought occurred to me.

"It was you guys who lit up our Internet connection wasn't it?" I remembered the momentary connection on the Internet the modem. I hadn't told Ruth Ann about it yet. "You already have a plan to make it work if we refuse to leave, don't you?"

"We can just take your equipment Walter."

"Then you don't get me."

"We can just take you too."

"Then you still don't me. I'll write ten thousand lines of nonsense code that won't do shit – you figure out what's wrong with it."

"We can make things difficult for you Walter. Think of Miss Goody Two Shoes."

"I'm thinking of her right now, asshole. You said you know what I did in California. Then you know we do it my way or we don't do it. Christmas Tree out."

I didn't switch off the radio – I just let it sit there. Ruth Ann was completely stunned.

"You pompous ass! Who do you think you are?" she demanded.

"I think I'm their only choice for something they need. Do you want to go to Lambeau Field? Do you want to be one of a herd of prey animals waiting to be eaten? If I'm wrong this radio won't make a peep. If I'm right, we'll hear Frank any minute now."

We waited. Ruth Ann reached for the mike. I shielded it from her. We waited.

"Walter, this is Frank. Are you listening?"

"Yes Frank."

"We'll do it your way. Our people will set you up."

"Thank you Frank. When your people get here have them bring a contract signed by whoever is in charge there. One page. No more. It has to say the government of the Administrative Zone will set us up, keep us supplied and keep us safe, both of us. In return, we rent you our equipment and provide consulting services. One page."

"OK Walter. A pleasure doing business with you." Frank's response dripped with sarcasm.

Ruth Ann asked "A contract? A contract? What do you need a contract for?"

"You remember that Lieutenant Mancheski, we signed a release to be left alone here. Remember the radio? It had an end user agreement on it. These people are bureaucrats hon. Bureaucrats live on paper. It's what they understand."

Ruth Ann folded her arms and cocked her head in skepticism and said "And you think a contract will keep us safe?"

"This is just business."

My belief in the continuance of government's old habits was borne out an hour later when the tactical radio began beeping. The small display window said a document had arrived in its drop box folder (where I still dumped pictures for transmission to Lambeau). I copied it over to my laptop and opened it up. It was a PDF file. Inside was a non-disclosure agreement.

I started laughing my head off and showed it to Ruth Ann. She gave me a fake laugh in return and walked away.

◆ During a scheduled meeting, Frank outlined briefly that the government had three initiatives they wanted help with.

Frank's people had a small number of developers among the refugees in Door County. There were some process control types from a paper mill, some numerical computation programmers from insurance companies and some general web types. None had executive or project leadership experience. I would be nominally "in charge" because of my management experience.

This was second nature.

If Frank's people, *my* people, were any good things would be easy. If they weren't I'd have Frank move their desks *outside* the protective perimeter of Lambeau field.

I would be facilitating one project and actually implementing the tricky parts of another. The third I'd get to when the first two were done.

Apart from military traffic I didn't know or care about, we were one of just a few dozen sites on the Internet. It was karma, I suppose. Several of the predecessors of the Internet ran through Wisconsin. In a way, this, like the hordes trampling Wisconsin, was full circle.

Getting Christmas Tree online meant some number of facilities digitally 'between" here and Lambeau Field had to be cleared of infection, powered up and defended. I am told there were casualties but I don't know the details. Later on, I asked Frank if people died because I refused to leave my house. He told me not to blame myself, which I took to mean "Yes."

Then he looked me directly in the eyes (we finally met when things settled down) and told me the work those people died doing had to be done anyway. Lambeau Field had to have the high-speed connectivity to be part of rebuilding command and control systems across the administrative zones.

And, he said, the work I did saved a lot of lives.

◆ In the afternoon, we listened to the radio update. It was like a Smothers Brothers comedy routine from the Ed Sullivan show. Good news. Bad news.

The good news was that Chicago B, the mega-horde had been pounded at the Rock River north of Janesville, south of Edgerton. The river had few crossings in the area and jutted out to the west making a nice pocket. Hundreds of thousands of undead had been incinerated. This made a dent in the horde's size though I doubt anyone in their path would count their lucky stars at being surrounded by 3.7 million dead versus 4 million.

The bad news was that the horde was now following Interstate 90 north. There would not be another significant natural choke point for fifty miles. In a little more than twenty miles, a day's trample, Chicago B would pass through Madison, where it all began.

The TC horde was southeast of the burned out remains of Eau Claire and Chippewa Falls Wisconsin. The good news was that it turned south, away from Door County.

The bad news was that the horde was traveling in line with Interstate 94, which, about eighty miles away, links with the very same Interstate 90 that the Chicago B mega-horde currently traveled. The possibility loomed that the two hordes would combine.

The TC horde had clear country for the next two days walk until they reached Black River Falls. Then, a waterway with limited crossings would bunch them up again.

◆ It snowed all day. It was beautiful, just as I had hoped. Virginal wet snowman making snow coated all surfaces including the undead that were standing still. They turned almost instantly into unattractive snowmen, too skinny and linear to be jolly. If Frosty had looked like these, the 'thumpetty thump thump" in the song would have been the sound of disconnecting Frosty's brain from his spinal column. Don't complain about my analogy. Shooting a snowman in the head to kill it makes as much sense as having to shoot dead people in their heads to kill them.

The snowmen near our house represented an opportunity to relieve some of the stress the last few days had induced. Ruth Ann's love of all things that fire projectiles included paintball. We had a CO2 paintball rifle with a store of cylinders and the paintballs themselves. We discussed having this bit of fun including its ramifications. We decided that a paintball rifle wouldn't be loud enough to pose much of a risk of attracting zombies from far and wide.

Just the same, Ruth Ann would forego her turns with the paintball rifle. Instead, she would be ready with her recurve bow to dispatch any snow cones that started making too much noise. Ryan, of course, already knew how to fire the paintball rifle but I needed instructions from Ruth Ann.

Pop! Ryan landed a bright magenta splotch on the shoulder blade of a statue on the house's southeast side near where we had shot the looters. The impact of the paintball jerked the ghoul to its front. It spun quickly around and growled in the direction the shot had come. It scanned left and right at its eye's level never lifting its head to explore what might be found above it. It shifted into that constant moaning that anyone who has heard never wants to hear again. It shambled off towards the back of the house and kept right on going now that it had been activated.

Emboldened by our success without apparent penalty, I took the next shot at a snow-covered ghoul. This one faced directly at our firing location but its eyes were obscured by snow. With beginner's luck on my side, I exploded a bright blue paintball directly into its face. The impact of the paintball removed the accumulated snow from its eyes which flashed upwards right at me while I was still visible admiring my shot.

The creature roared and moved with purpose towards the house. Ruth Ann nocked her bow, drew and put an arrow between the creature's eyes. It fell cleanly backwards with its arms outstretched. Momentum from the fall brought its arms to rest spread eagle. There was now a snow angel with a bright blue face on my lawn.

The snow angel's roar brought two walkers in our direction. Ryan took his turn, putting the paintball rifle on automatic. Letting the first howling walker get closer, he made modern art on the creature's torso and face.

More creatures started in our direction. The adult in me decided this is where the fun was transitioning to the part where you get the sharp stick in the eye. The adult in me was overruled by the stressed out me that needed just a bit more release. I sprayed the second ghoul on automatic making the two coming towards us some kind of animated diptych.

"OK, we better stop. We've had our fun," the adult using my voice said.

"That was great!" Ryan said too loudly.

Ruth Ann's contribution to the discussion was two quick bowshots, putting the natty pair down with holes in their heads.

We quietly got down off the roof. Once down to the second floor we made hot chocolate and tea. We felt a bit of relief from the horrors of a horde passing through our yard. With the cold weather and lack of continued stimulation, the group that accumulated at our house slowly wandered away or deactivated into statues.

◆ On Wednesday (Day 35), a number of Blackhawks arrived. The first two erupted with combat teams upon setting down. The troops began methodically eliminating all of the undead in the area. We did not hear any shots from their suppressed weapons. Their teams moved like water rushing downhill pausing in one spot only long enough to place aimed fire on groups of undead. They took out individual zombies while on the move without breaking stride.

When they came upon a home that was compromised, they simply laid charges around its periphery, fired M203 grenades in through whatever breach the ghouls had made and blew the house up. Anything that moved was shot. There was no sense in risking lives on clearing tight spaces. It occurred to me that I had designed my home to survive the others in the neighborhood. I thought it would be acts of nature that brought them down not explosives.

A third Blackhawk disgorged a smaller combat team that swept into the Boetche's house. In less than a minute, they confirmed its contents were secure. A large twin rotor helicopter landed next to the house. A crew went inside and then shortly came out again carting bales of dope and boxes of equipment. Before the outbreak, this sort of scene would appear on the news from time to time with DEA emblazoned in big letters on the chests and backs of law enforcement. Now instead of a crime, it was a weed rescue mission.

With a short but earnest goodbye, Ryan left on the cargo chopper.

After clearing an extended area of undead, one of the first two teams set up a protective perimeter around us. The other team used bailing hooks to make a pile of undead from those killed in the area of our house. They set the pile ablaze. The stink was terrible. The smoking pyre destroyed what was left of the illusion of normalcy the snow had brought.

More cargo helicopters arrived. One suspended what looked like a steel shipping container under it. Another suspended a pallet carrying a Bobcat with various doodads attached. A third cargo helicopter landed first. Crewmembers jumped out and guided the soft touchdown of the suspended cargo carried by the other two.

The shipping container was put down near where our deck used to be, very close and parallel to the house. After laying down their loads both choppers that carried the heavy cargo departed without landing.

The ramp door of the remaining cargo helicopter came down and men walked out with 4x8 sheets of thick plywood. They set the wood down at the front door. Other men set up a portable table saw and small gas powered generator. With a hook, they pulled the dead ghoul out of the front door's sidelight and added it to the pyre that was still roaring with flame. They cut and screwed the plywood completely over my front entry way then added metal gussets anchoring the wood to the concrete further reinforcing the heavy sheets.

Meanwhile, the Bobcat removed pallets of heavy metal fencing from the belly of the remaining cargo chopper. Men went to work on the shipping container that housed a complete fuel cell electrical generator powered by natural gas. The system was of modest size incorporating fuel storage, the fuel cell system itself and the electrical glue necessary to convert the output of the container to levels compatible with the input of the house.

All told, the fuel cell system could provide fifty times the capacity of our solar panels with enough natural gas to run a month. Workers tied the output of the fuel cell to the input of the house so to us, it was like being reconnected to the grid again. As a bonus, we could continue using our rooftop panels at the same time to keep our batteries conditioned and charged. We would have enough electricity to run the servers in the basement plus heaters, a refrigerator, freezer, microwave and coffee maker all at the same time!

The fuel cell system had the capacity to heat water as a byproduct, but the work involved in ducting and piping was deemed frivolous. Hot showers would not return to Christmas Tree. Can't have everything.

The heavy metal fencing was anchored to the concrete of the walls of my house. Then sections were linked together with pins. Then the pins and gaps between the sections were welded. Buttresses extended to the inside of the fence giving it increased resistance from outside forces pushing inward. I was not happy having something that zombies could climb so close to the house but they seemed to know what they were doing.

Finally, a sloped metal cage was placed over the cleared off top of our wellhead. Frank's people, who knew our house's weaknesses from watching the TC horde come through, were thinking of everything.

When construction was done for the day, the cargo helicopter attached the Bobcat to fly it, and the construction crews back to Door County. It was then that I made believe I was exercising my (suspended) third amendment rights. The third amendment guarantees that no troops can be quartered in private homes without the owner's consent.

A full squad of soldiers assembled near my garage door. After numerous assurances that the virus was no longer transmittable via proximity, we admitted eleven heavily armed infantrymen into Camp Christmas Tree. Not all of the men were strangers. Lieutenant Mancheski, the Guardsman we declined to go with almost three weeks before shook our hands as he brought his people in. A Staff Sergeant named Orderly presented Ruth Ann with two washed mason jars with her hand written "strawberry" still visible. "It went fast ma'am. We didn't know if you needed the jars back. I'm sorry about the other two jars. We lost them but not without a fight."

Ruth Ann was genuinely touched. She thanked Sergeant Orderly for returning the jars. A short time before two glass jars would not be worth the effort to carry back. Now however…

Lieutenant Mancheski handed me an envelope. Inside was a signed contract with the terms I had specified.

The men began to make themselves comfortable in the bedrooms and den on our first floor. With ample electricity, water was not a problem. The soldiers came supplied with food. Periodic resupply was part of the deal.

They pulled Ryan's 4x4 out of our garage and parked it in the Boetche's garage. They set up a more comfortable sleeping area in the vacated space. Lt. Mancheski explained this would be used as a quarantine area if one proved necessary. Until used for that purpose, the garage's back door would serve as the main entrance and egress point for the house.

He defined a duty schedule that put four soldiers on our roof twenty-four hours a day. A fifth would keep watch of the security cameras and monitor the radio.

Lt. Mancheski asked if there was anything his men could do for us. It didn't take much thought. Both Ruth Ann and I answered we wanted to go out for a long walk! The Lieutenant said that could be arranged for the next day. The remainder of this day needed to be spent on setting up and settling in.

I took Lt. Mancheski, Sgt. Orderly and the squad's tech person Specialist Brandt for a complete tour of the house instructing them on each of the system's operation and capability. They were quite satisfied with the house's defensibility especially under a state of siege.

SPC Brandt correctly pointed out that for all my concern about survivability, I had no way to protect the vital assets I had on the roof: the solar array and greenhouse.

"Ah, that," I said. "I considered them expendable. Their only protection is a homeowner's insurance policy. Not that that would do much good anymore."

"I resemble that remark Mr. Handsman," said the Lieutenant. "Before this I worked out of the office that serviced your policy. So, in a roundabout way, we still have you covered."

"Small world! If I recall correctly my policy premium would have been due about now. Would you accept payment in the form of brandied pears? You've had Ruth Ann's jam, the pears are even better."

Sgt. Orderly shook like an excited kid and said, "LT please say yes."

"As I am temporarily out of touch with the home office, I'm sure we can work out an arrangement," he said with a smile.

"Good. Now show me this nuclear reactor you guys installed."

Orderly thought I was serious and said, "It's a fuel cell system Mr. Handsman, there are no nuclear things in there."

When we had exited the back door, I heard sounds emanating from the machine. There was both a 60-cycle noise common to generators and high-pitched hissing. I commented on the hissing.

Specialist Brandt said, "That's the sound of the natural gas working through from its tanks through the system."

"Isn't that pretty loud? It isn't going to attract any zombies?"

"We don't think so."

"What do you mean *think so?* Haven't you tried this before?"

"Actually, no sir. This is the first time we have deployed a unit of this kind in the open field."

"Great." Be careful what you wish for, I thought to myself.

We made our way inside and broke open some brandied pears. A number of jars actually. Being the caring soul that my stone cold executioner wife is, she made paper plates full for the troops on the roof.

That evening I fired up the servers and confirmed connectivity with Lambeau Field. Our connection speed was phenomenal with minimal latency. The first items on my "to do" list included setting up a means of communicating with not only Frank but also the people I would ostensibly be supervising. A secure email account that Frank's people provided took only a moment to setup. I fired up an enterprise collaboration server that would let me host live meetings with "my people." However, I never did get the damn thing working correctly. We ended up using only email.

Among the first emails I received were instructions on how to tie into a feed of high-resolution satellite imagery covering the Midwestern Administrative Zone. The first project I would be working on needed these. I arranged to pull down new set of high-res images every fifteen minutes. I would begin writing code to process these images soon. For tonight however, Ruth Ann and I simply looked at them, one stream in visible light and one in infrared.

Being nighttime, the visual light images showed very little, far less than they used to. There were giant expanses of darkness that were once lit by human activity. The infrared images showed fairly little as well. Residual heat from the day mostly. There were some bright spots in the pictures. These were recent fires or possibly small encampments of humans. Door County shone very brightly. There was even a glow around my house, which I found by latitude and longitude.

The hordes did not show up to the naked eye in the infrared stream but I was told it would be possible to spot them using computer code to identify their minor difference from the background. Spotting them at night was some of the code I was asked to write.

◆ Thursday (Day 36), was the start of a new phase in our survival story. My house was now a military installation of sorts officially called Camp Christmas Tree named after how we lit of the night with our infrared floodlights. Ruth Ann and I had our own squad of hardened zombie killers to protect us. This morning, we went for a walk.

Ruth Ann and I talked with the Lieutenant and Sgt. Orderly. As we chit chatted about this and that they politely kept their automatic weapons pointed in another direction. Fifteen yards away from us, spread like the cardinal points on a compass were four more soldiers armed more heavily than those beside us.

The sound of soft snow crunching underfoot and quiet but lively conversation intermingled with an occasional moan followed by the exhale of a suppressed assault rifle.

It was quite idyllic really.

Our companions told us of their escape from the fallen safe zone at Chippewa Valley Regional Airport a little more than two weeks before.

"At first we really thought we could pick a spot of ground and hold it. Come on, bullets and bombs against fingernails and teeth? Where's the challenge in that?" Lieutenant Mancheski began.

"We even went out on patrols looking for them when all we had to do was ring a dinner bell and they'd find us. Stealth wasn't an option for us like you have here. We had too many people at the airport to keep hidden."

"Puh." I saw the soldier to our right lower his suppressed rifle. I did not see the undead he just put down, lost in a row of evergreens ahead of us.

"Dispatchers from the local law enforcement branches did a great job of keeping our patrols in places with escape routes and where we could support each other. One weakness in this was that the dispatch centers were too far apart and their buildings too large to defend. When we lost them, one by one, we lost our command and control. The patrols *had* to stop. Offense with our limited resources was out of the question," he continued.

"Orderly here was on one of the last patrols. They were literally chased back into our perimeter."

"We had .50 cals on Humvees. We had our weapons and side arms but not a single suppressed weapon between us. Every time we nailed one son of a bitch, the noise brought another ten to take its place. Sometimes we made it back to the safe zone with a round still left in the chamber, sometimes we didn't. That last time, we came back empty and winded," the Sargent added. "It was frustrating. Every time out, more of them. Less of us."

"The worst were the people in the safe zone who got sick. At first, we pulled them away from their families to put them down. After a while, we could not risk even that. We executed parents and children in front of each other," the Lieutenant's voice cracked a little. His eyes were fixed on the horizon.

"Puh."

"When it was clear that we couldn't hold our line we had about eighteen hours that we could fly people out on small planes. It was like the English at Dunkirk. Little planes as few as three passengers at a time. The biggest plane, Orderly, what was it like five passengers plus the pilot?" Orderly nodded.

"We had three Gatling guns dropped in. We could have used more but that's all we could get. Three couldn't cover all of both of runways, so the planes had to climb out or land in shorter and shorter lengths. Then we couldn't hold even that. We continued the evac with choppers but soon we couldn't hold the clear patch off 90th street," Mancheski went on.

"We started moving people across the river but we didn't have enough boats. We strung ropes across the river to help people swim across. We used what boats we had for the little kids and elderly and to catch people downstream who couldn't hold on. Choppers on the other side lifted all the civilians out in the end."

"If the other side of the river wasn't just farms, we'd have been overrun for sure," Orderly said. "The road trip to Door County was no picnic. We had to go north around the bigger cities and come down on 43 to cross the Fox River. Going through Green Bay was awful. We kept the lake to our left and air cover made the difference on the right. We'd be walkers too if it weren't for that."

"Puh."

◆ A Blackhawk landing back at the house told us it was time to head home. Some workers had arrived to finish yesterday's miraculous conversion of our house into Camp Christmas Tree.

When we got back, it was work time for me too. The first project to work on would to be hosted on my traditional Linux servers. The ex-financial programmers in Door County worked for some of Wisconsin's well-known insurance companies. They were experts in the field of optimization.

Given a number of constraints plus a number of parameters, they wrote programs that optimized for a particular goal. For example, they might use medical data as constraints. Age, gender, smoking and alcohol use might be the parameters to vary. Their output might be insurance premiums that maximized the company's profit while keeping their rates in line with competitors.

It was not too far a stretch to apply their knowledge to taking terrain as constraints and horde movement as parameters. Their results would be optimized targeting plans for thinning operations.

As you know, the hordes were too big for men with rifles to make a dent. Heavier ordinance had to be used. For bombs and missiles to be used most effectively, the ghouls have to be packed together. Wounding does not help. Only a completely shredded body or decapitated head is any use.

So far, thinning operations tended to take place at the banks of rivers and lakes because they effectively slow a horde's progress until the creatures start squeezing over bridges or other crossings. The problem is there aren't enough rivers and lakes to allow the military to hit the hordes frequently enough. Going back to the Munz, Hudea, Imad and Smith zombie apocalypse paper:

"Only sufficiently frequent attacks, with increasing force, will result in eradication, assuming the available resources can be mustered in time."

It was imperative that more terrain features be leveraged as choke points. More choke points mean attacking more frequently satisfying every aspect of Munz et al.

Identifying less obvious choke points required fine grain modeling of horde movement and terrain. Because of these programmers' work, thinning operations took place more frequently and efficiently. It was a numbers game we had no choice but to win.

To get their analysis system running I had to script data wrangling code and create a job input and scheduling mechanism. Their code was up and running, producing results by early the next morning. Their input data still included handmade estimates of horde size and position however. Processes that include hand-made data can't be scaled to massive levels. I would be writing the code to analyze satellite pictures directly, both daytime and nighttime, to provide size, speed and direction data without human input.

◆ The country's scientific eggheads may have begun redeeming themselves today. Survivors down in the Gulf region include experts in oil-spill remediation techniques. They knew how to grow oil-eating microbes, even ones that work at the low temperatures found in the deep ocean. They wondered what they could trick the bacteria into doing on undead matter.

They brought their idea to their Administrative Zone who made it possible for their research to take place. The research, after a few experiments, showed enough promise to make today's radio broadcast. Either the report was true or it was propaganda to pump a little sunshine out to a demoralized and shrinking populace. In either case, the idea seemed plausible.

At the end of a thinning operation, after fresh wounds had been inflicted on the undead, an aerosol of the modified bacteria would be released. Landing on newly exposed dead meat, the bugs were supposed to speed up rotting even in temperatures down into the 30's.

The environmental impact of the spray was not known yet. That living test people didn't die immediately on exposure was good enough for wartime use.

Here "up north" we were already below freezing so the new development couldn't help us. But, assuming the report were true and the bugs could be grown in large quantities so there would be enough to go around, it would mean an early spring of sorts in northern latitudes.

That evening Lieutenant Mancheski's personal radio beeped.

"Six this is two, over."

"Go ahead two."

"LT there are two Zekes stumbling towards the back of the house. Permission to engage?"

"Affirmative two. Taken them down."

"Hooah six," heard, understood and acknowledged. A moment later:

"Six this is two. Zekes down sir."

"Very well. Six out."

◆ On Friday (Day 37), I started work on the image processing software needed to measure horde size, speed, and direction from satellite images. This was not very hard to do slowly. The idea is this: establish a baseline of what an area looked like before a horde arrived. The baseline allowed the software to filter out changes due to wind blowing trees, shifting shadows and the like. Then as the horde arrived, compare the new pictures to the baseline. Based upon differences exceeding a certain threshold, a tiny spot on the ground was covered by zombies or not. A slightly more subtle step was figuring out the contour of the horde itself. Then, counting up the number of occupied picture elements (pixels) and subtracting from the total inside the contour gave a pretty good estimate of the horde's number. Finally, monitoring the progress of the contour itself gave physical size, speed and direction with even finer data being available to pinpoint what parts of a horde were more densely packed that others.

To make this algorithm run fast so that larger and larger swaths of ground could be analyzed was harder. To do it, I converted standard computing code into massively parallel programs that ran on the small supercomputer I had. Supercomputers aren't called super for nothing. Even my small supercomputer ate this kind of processing for breakfast. After a full day at it, my code could process pictures far faster than the optimization code could figure out where to attack. I added traditional servers built from old parts lying around to help in equalizing the system so that no cycles went to waste.

After a few hours gaining experience with the system's performance, whoever was in charge of such things authorized Christmas Tree to receive satellite data from other Administrative Zones.

Camp Christmas Tree had shifted quietly from being tactically important to strategically important.

Spotting hordes at night proved straightforward. Taking deeper statistics from baseline images and comparing these to the current feeds, meant cold zombies.

Day and night now, the military had fine-grained data on horde location, speed, direction, size and density. Thinning operations could be conducted around the clock using just the right resources for each unique set of conditions.

Ruth Ann and I took a good look at the Chicago B horde and a few others around the country. At more than three million strong, Chicago B was terrifying. We're not religious. Just the same we prayed Chicago B would stay away from us.

Chicago B wasn't the largest horde around. Ruth Ann and I saw a comprehensive picture of what was going on around the country that probably no one else outside the top brass would see until historians got access to the same data.

"Well, now we know how much filtering goes on in the radio updated," Ruth Ann said. "We aren't being told anything about how bad things are around the major cities."

Information was being very limited indeed.

It was a good day's work and my basement data center was humming.

◆ In a symbolic but meaningful gesture, the workers here today cored out a hole in the frozen ground and planted a thirty-foot pole. On it flew the Star Spangled Banner. Having read our story this far you would be correct if you assumed that before all this I would not have given two shits about flying a flag, especially on *my* lawn.

Now though I almost cried when I came up for air from programming. Ruth Ann and I hugged each other tightly as we watched the flag wave in the wind. I was driven to tears. Was it love of country or indignation at the destruction being wrought upon it? I don't know. I felt good to see the symbol.

Given what contribution Christmas Tree was making to the war effort, to me the flag shouted, "You can walk but you can't hide. You have come after us long enough. Now we're coming after you."

◆ Several times during the day Bill Mancheski's radio beeped to announce walkers, in ones and twos approaching the back of the house. I was with the Lieutenant when one call came. I motioned to him that I'd like to say something before he replied on the radio.

"Can you ask them what direction the Zekes are coming from when the see one approaching the house?"

"Three, this is six."

"Whenever a Zeke approaches the house please say from which direction they are coming and to which direction they are going. Pass it on. Hooah?"

I heard four mike clicks, one for each soldier on the roof.

"Three, say directions for the Zekes so far."

"The ones we have put down today have come no direction in particular. They all appeared to be heading towards the back of the house."

I motioned to Bill again my desire to speak.

"Hold three."

"Can you ask them to let them get close to the house before dropping them? They are all heading to the back of the house. Let's see where at the back of the house."

"All, this is six. We want to see where they are heading specifically. Let Zeke get close and report."

◆ There was no doubt about it any longer. On Saturday (Day 38), anyone looking at the progress of the TC and CB hordes walking Wisconsin could see they were going to merge around Mauston by tomorrow. So much for the power of prayer.

"What's going to happen when they merge?" Ruth Ann began.

"I don't think they are going to have a rumble like the Sharks and the Jets," I said while trying to think of something more likely. "The one from Illinois is now about three times larger than the one from Minnesota. I think just the momentum of the Chicago horde alone will drag the smaller horde back north. Towards us."

"Looks like Christmas Tree will be in the center of another stampede," Bill Mancheski added. "We have about a week to get ready."

"Maybe it's time to get out of here?" said Ruth Ann.

"What? Bill just got here. Lambeau just invested a ton of resources in us."

"Doug, you're talking like we're some startup that just got funded. This is our lives we're talking about. We should be thinking about leaving. Hell, we should be leaving, period."

"I wouldn't worry too much hon. We survived a horde once and now we're even better off than before. Tell her Bill."

"I'm sorry Doug. I go where they tell me."

"Well, I'm not going anywhere. Lambeau needs our results right *now*. The whole country needs our results. There's more code I have to write. I can't write code while I'm packing up, flying to Lambeau and unpacking. Shit, half the equipment wouldn't make the trip and turn on again. Where do we get replacement parts? It would at least a day maybe two to get running again if we even can get running again," I was pretty adamant.

"You're playing with our lives now Doug."

"Hon, I have been since the day we got married. Besides, you should trust me. I work for the government." My joke did not go over well.

◆ Later in the day I saw a new configuration file come down from Lambeau for the thinning optimizer. I had to restart the system to incorporate the new settings. By email from one of my people, I got the low down on the new download.

"We added modeling for aerial dropped land mines. Mauston is perfect for them."

I checked the maps. They were right. East of Mauston is a waterway. West of Mauston is the some of the most uneven terrain in all of Wisconsin, the hills and bluffs of the Driftless Area formed more than 500,000 years ago. In between was a flat plain through which CB would be soon shuffling.

I wrote back:

"How much area are they thinking of mining?"

I got back:

"All of it."

Ah, well. Land mines make a lot of sense but they hadn't been used in the U.S. up until now. They are known throughout the world as the gift that keeps on giving. Once that area was mined, it was likely it would remain a no man's land for decades. Once again, whom am I kidding? The land is a no man's land already.

In addition, the U.S. had resisted treaties for years banning land mines. We had more mines than anyone else. The higher ups figured if we have them, might as well use them.

Within a half an hour our analysis system confirmed the area was great for a thinning operation when the new weapon system, aerial mines, was added to the palette.

In another hour, the satellite feed captured formations of planes over the area. In another hour after that, helicopters crisscrossed the plain south of Mauston, north of Wisconsin Dells.

Aerial mines are anti-personnel weapons. They are intended to maim not necessarily kill. It was unlikely that the weapons would destroy many brainstems but it would make several tightly packed zombies immobile per mine detonated. A zombie with no legs is still dangerous. However, it is a danger confined to a fixed and known area. The accountants of destruction could calculate then to take them out or just let them rot where they lay.

It was just as well that the CB horde was many hours away from the field. There were so many mines that the planning system needed new baseline images to account for the change in color of the land.

On the radio, our troops were said to be on the move again in Door County and Puerto Rico. Sealing underground tunnels brought a dramatic decrease in recurrences of outbreak.

The day's bad news was that it was now demonstrated fact that the ghouls continued functioning underwater. No horde had wandered en mass into a large body of water like the Atlantic or even the Great Lakes. Attacks being recorded now in disinfected areas of Door County and Puerto Rico were sporadic and easily put down if they were spotted quickly. The key was spotting them quickly as they came up out of the water. Coastlines are too long to station troops that were needed elsewhere. Civilian "Coastal Defense Forces" were being organized. Their effectiveness was uneven, especially at night.

I could help with that.

I fished out some old articles on using the Raspberry Pi for stereo vision off my NAS. I grabbed two webcams and attached them to one Pi. I pointed them roughly in the same direction toed in a little bit. After confirming I had pictures from both and I started writing code.

The first part of the code was essentially the same as I had written the day before. Some swath of coastline such as a beach, for example, should have no one on it, that's key. Baseline images told the code where to filter out any windblown grasses and continuous motion like waves. If something is spotted moving, the two eyes are compared and with some judicious use of trigonometry the angle and distance to the object could be accurately determined (once distances had been calibrated during setup). I demonstrated this to Bill Mancheski and Sgt. Orderly by having the system place a crosshair over a third soldier automatically as he wandered around outside.

Both Bill and I had a conference with Frank and others at Lambeau to explain what I built and how it could be used. I reminded Frank he had access to process control engineers that could easily write code to take the crosshair data I generated and control servos to aim and fire a weapon. Even if it didn't fire a weapon it could send a warning message that something was moving where it shouldn't be (if some type of ad hoc wireless network were available).

Prior to the war, this type of contraption would set the government back a hundred grand from a defense contractor. Now, apart from the weapon, we could build them for under three hundred bucks in parts: computer, cameras, servos, stands, recharger and batteries all for a price less than an afternoon's bar bill from the defense industry.

The system had no failsafe in it though. Once it was set, there was no way to walk in front of one without being shot. This was an acceptable flaw for the time being and could be corrected over time.

A Blackhawk came later that day to drop supplies and take most of my Pi's back to Lambeau while they figured out where to find more. Pi's had been created in England to help children around the world learn about technology. I had purchased them to give to middle school children here in town. They would be used to help children after all. Help them avoid being eaten.

I ended the radio conference with Lambeau by adding that it would be a trivial change to connect the output of the Pi's to M18 Claymore directional antipersonnel mines. These mines can blast ball bearings over two hundred feet without hurting what is behind them. I suggested they mount the mines at head height on telephone poles or similarly sized trees. I told them to set the Pi up on the "far" side with cameras out on stalks. My guys up in Door County could modify the code to fire the Claymore when a certain sized movement was spotted so groups of zombies could be killed instead of the first one that wandered by.

My thinking was that this sort of device could be parachuted into small camps to help in their defense or used by troops for delaying actions.

Lambeau was excited by my development. I told them it was all included as part of my service.

The work I supposed to do for the day was interrupted when I saw unusual behavior on my servers running the optimization code.

What was it a couple of days at most these things were running? I found the anomaly in the form of a massive Minecraft server that appeared to have several hundred users when I shut it down.

I had a second conference with just Frank and told him which of my people left behind his digital fingerprints. Fortunately, it was a junior engineer. He assured me the person would be disciplined. I don't know what Frank did but I never had a problem with my servers again.

We also had enough zombies approach the back of the house to know where they were going, or wanted to go. Every single one approached the back and stopped near the natural gas end of the fuel cell system. When they got up against the protective fence some banged on it, others entered statue mode. Sometimes the statues would stop behind the fuel cell container where the soldiers could not get a clear shot. They had to yell and make a commotion to get the statues to wake up, walk a few feet over so they could be shot.

I reported this to Frank in our last conversation of the day.

"Have any of these fuel systems been deployed in the field, Frank? Like we have here with just a fence, no protected perimeter?" I said.

"Negative Christmas Tree. You're the first."

"Well, there might be a problem with keeping them out where walkers can congregate. Lieutenant can you fill Frank in on what we've seen today?"

"Sir, we have observed walkers arrive from all directions and congregate at the natural gas end of the fuel cell system. From the roof, my men can't smell any gas leaks. I sent a man down to ground level, he reported no smell of gas there either. There is the constant hissing from the gas moving from its tank into the system. Zeke seems to be drawn to it, sir."

"Understood Christmas Tree. I will have somebody look into that. Anything else?"

Bill and I exchanged looks.

"Nothing else Lambeau, Christmas Tree out."

◆ Around 10:30 PM, I reconfigured the satellite feed covering Wisconsin to download a new IR image once per minute. I wanted to see the yield from the mining of Mauston. I hooked the HDMI output of my laptop up to our big screen TV, which thankfully still worked. With the lights down to a minimum, Ruth Ann and I along with all the soldiers off duty gathered around the TV for the show.

First I showed the crowd the glowing dots from Camp Christmas Tree for perspective, then traced southeast about 120 miles to where the Dells / Mauston area is.

We did not have to wait very long.

At the first new glowing dot, the soldiers cheered. Then, with each new image, the glowing dots moved in a slow wave extending further and further northwest. The horde was marching right through the densely laid minefield. As their front ranks detonated mines, the following ranks just kept walking. We saw a widening line of dots that ultimately stretched west from the Wisconsin River all the way to the hills of the Driftless Area almost ten miles away.

The ripple of dots began showing a bulge that slowly formed into a wedge shape pointing along Interstate 90/94. As the horde marched deeper into the minefield the width of the glowing dots shrunk. The dead, without any kind of cognition, were forming up behind a spearhead of their leading edge. While some dots winked in and out to the east and west of the horde's advance, the brightest glows continued to be along the Interstate.

Unbeknownst to us, helicopters on Lambeau Field's orders were orbiting the area from high above. With night vision gear they shot video zoomed in close enough to see individual ghouls get thrown like bowling pins and pinballs combined. One of my guys sent me an email with a clip from the helicopters cameras. I put it up on the TV and my guests howled with approval.

After putting the live feed back on I wandered over to the kitchen. I found Ruth Ann there nursing some tea. I joined her.

"The carnage is horrible," she said. "But those aren't people. We're doing them a favor."

"Yes, we are."

"Is it cutting down the size of CB?"

"Definitely, but I don't think it's doing as good a job as our friends here think. The dead are lining up to follow a path of least resistance. Further from the highway that place will be dangerous for years."

"How many do you think we're getting?"

"I don't know yet. My code is thrown off by the constantly moving wave of detonations and heat differences caused by the explosions. I won't be able to give an accurate number until daylight."

"We should leave Doug. Leave now before the hordes come back."

"We talked about this hon. We made it through once, we'll make it through again."

"I don't think so babe. I hope I turn first so I can bite the shit out of you."

"Hon, if you turn first you will have no problem at all getting shit out of me. I'll do it all by myself."

We went to bed.

◆ On Sunday (Day 39), the thinning optimizer placed the size of TC at 1.1 million and CB at 2.5 million. About 800,000 zombies had been immobilized in the minefield last night. I zoomed into the satellite images south of Mauston and saw a veritable moonscape of small densely packed craters. I subtracted some consecutive images from each other and saw pixels changing everywhere. As expected, many zombies weren't completely de-animated but neither could they move around much.

In my mind's eye, I could picture a scene from Soylent Green someday taking place north of the Waterpark Capital of the World. I could imagine front loaders moving slowly across the moonscape scooping up wriggling zombies and dumping them into waiting dump trucks. What would be done with all that organic matter? I don't know but I bet if we put enough of them together in one place and wait sixty million years, we'll strike oil.

I was talking the numbers over with Bill.

"We started at over six million in two hordes. When they combine, we'll be down to 3,600,000 in one horde after eleven days of non-stop attacks," I said.

"And to get down that far we left fifty square miles uninhabitable due to land mines. We're wearing out our people and equipment. Brandt is telling me he is hearing of more and more downed helos and planes. This kind of sustained action requires repair and replenishment. Seems to me the spare parts department at Sikorsky factory is closed."

"You know it's going to shift back onto your shoulders don't you? I don't mean you personally, but ground troops. It's going to shift back onto you guys."

"It always does, but why do you say that?"

"The whole concept of the TOs are to thin, right? Well, once the hordes are thinned to the point that low density means dropping bombs is ineffective, we'll be back to door-to-door and hand to hand. By "we" I mean you, no offense."

"None taken. I actually wouldn't mind being out in the field again. There's only so many times I can strip and clean my weapon. My men are restless. You've got a nice house and all, but we'd rather be on the move. No offense."

"None taken. Ruth Ann is convinced we're screwed by staying here."

"She might be right. Your fortress has a second floor with holes that are way too big. I would be more comfortable in a medieval castle with arrow slits. These glass windows up here, they will go in a heartbeat if the dead press against them."

"How is that going to happen? We're on a second floor."

"It can happen. If they're motivated, they'll climb on top of each other. It can happen."

I parted from Bill almost too disturbed to work on what I needed to do for the day.

Fortunately, what I needed to do was easy. Lambeau field needed web hosts and database systems to be able to share data more effectively. I took two physical servers out of the rotation of those working on the thinning optimizer without losing any functionality. Each had twin CPUs with four cores each. This is almost like having sixteen computers on just the two boards.

It goes up even from there. I fired up a "virtual computing" environment allowing multiple make believe computers to run on one physical computer. This works because only some of the make believe computers will be busy at the same time. The benefit of having all the make believe computers is that each can be handed over to its own web master or administrator who would then be free to screw it up without breaking all the other make believe computers.

In all, I instanced one hundred sixty make believe computers and sent the access details up to Lambeau.

This task, though important, only took a few hours of my time. Once I had the first make believe computer set up I could walk away while the others built were automatically.

Ruth Ann was out hunting with some of Bill's men. We finally figured out what happened to all the animals.

They're still out there.

They had evolved to avoid all sorts of predators more intelligent and faster than the undead. Wherever the undead were, animals weren't. Why didn't we humans think of that?

In her absence, I watched the merging of TC and CB. It was exactly like watching simulations of galaxies merge. As I expected, the axis of march shifted in the direction of the bigger horde. In a little over three hours it was done. The combined horde was christened Chicago B2, or CB2. It was headed right back at us.

From the time TC passed us to the time it merged with CB to make CB2, the Twin Cities horde had gone from 1.6 million to 1.1 million or a decrease of about a third. CB2 had to march back up along the same path route to get back here. It stands to reason, I thought, that we could expect about a third to be killed off before CB2 got here, right?

So, running the numbers to make myself feel better I estimated that CB2 would number about 2.4 million by the time it walked onto my lawn.

I didn't feel better.

A half an hour later the thinning optimizer spit out an opportunity. CB2 had forked a smaller group that stayed to the west of Decorah Lake. They were now bunched up especially tight against the bluffs and were being left behind by CB2. Barely twenty minutes later planes began bombing this splinter. Helicopter gunships that arrived after the planes had left engaged the remaining dead with Gatling guns and missiles. It would be ground troops next, exactly as Bill and I discussed earlier in the day.

"See?" I said to myself, "down to 3,400,000 already."

Things were looking up.

Except they weren't.

The center of mass of CB2 was heading northwest at an average of more than two miles an hour, double the speed of the hordes marching over fresh ground. Maybe they could tell there was nothing left alive where they were so they could move faster. Maybe they were getting hungrier. Nobody knew.

The reality was we would have a far shorter time to prepare for CB2 than we expected. Bill and Ruth Ann seemed quite sure we wouldn't survive CB2. My own self-doubt grew by the hour.

It certainly didn't help that walking dead were, in dribs and drabs, appearing out of the tree lines and fields that surrounded us. When the soldiers on the roof let them get close, they invariably headed for the back of the house. Something about the fuel cell system was drawing them in.

◆ That evening an event took place that unsettled things even more. I was in the kitchen enjoying some tea with Ruth Ann and Bill. I hadn't had the courage yet to tell them about the increase in CB2's speed. I had to tell them, it was critical that I did, and I was about to when I got an email from one of my guys in Lambeau. It said I should look the output of the thinning optimizer's last run for Wisconsin.

"Endres at Lambeau wants me to take a look at something," I said, opening a laptop at the table. "Let's see what Jay's got in the box, shall we?" I said.

"Who is Jay?" Bill said.

"Who was Jay. Jay was this guy who went around surprising your parents and grandparents with diamond rings and llamas."

"Oh. That explains everything. So what does Jay have in the box?"

"A llama."

"Doug, you're confusing us," said Ruth Ann impatiently.

"It's the next thinning operation in Wisconsin. It isn't for CB2. There's another horde on the move. The thinning operation is for the Mequon area. On I-43."

"What? That's on the lakefront."

"Yeah, a horde has formed up and left Milwaukee. It's heading north on the highway that leads straight to Lambeau. It's 90 miles from Door County."

"That puts the horde there on Thursday," Bill said.

"That's not all that's happening on Thursday.

"What now?" said Ruth Ann.

"CB2, it's walking twice as fast as we've seen it before. It will be here too on Thursday. Around the same time in fact."

Bill's eyes grew wide.

"Shit Doug, we have to get out of here." Ruth Ann demanded.

"OK hon. I'll ask Frank to schedule a pickup when I talk to him in the morning."

"About fucking time," Ruth Ann stormed off.

Bill left to brief his men.

◆ When I talked to Frank on Monday morning (Day 40), he was not in a good mood.

"So we're up to a million, is that right? They're headed right at us."

"Yeah, they are south of Sheboygan right now. The optimizer called for a strike about 20 minutes ago."

"I know. Planes are heading out now. There aren't a lot of them. Most of our birds are grounded for maintenance. We're calling for more planes from carrier task forces in the Atlantic but the ones they can spare don't pack the same punch. A RORO resupply ship is bringing replacement parts so we should be back to full fixed wing strength in a day."

"And helicopters?"

"Same. Most are down for maintenance. We should be back up to strength in a day. We're not going to be able to throw much at CB2. The horde marching on Lambeau takes precedence."

"Frank… This makes my request more urgent. We want to be evacuated."

"Now? You're kidding me, right Walter? You busted our chops to stay out there in the middle of nowhere and now you want to bug out? I've got a quick answer for you. No."

"Why not?"

"Isn't it obvious? Milwaukee A is bearing down on the only protection 300,000 Americans have, our forces are depleted and in need of rest, repair and resupply, and you know what else?"

"What?"

"You're too important. The results coming out of Christmas Tree are too vital to be without right now. We can't afford it. Not just here. You're computers are identifying strike opportunities across half the country. You'll be fine."

"Frank you committed to keeping us safe."

"And at this moment you are safe. The horizon on which we can plan is getting shorter and shorter. Right now, you're staying put."

The conversation with Frank ended abruptly.

◆ The first raid on MA (Milwaukee A) took place at Port Washington, Wisconsin. There was a choke point there between the Milwaukee River to the west and Lake Michigan to the east. It destroyed the town.

The need to cut down the size of MA was so acute that all the Milwaukee River crossings were destroyed. Even though the river was fairly wide, about 80,000 undead crossed the waterway. They would likely lose their connection to the horde and be cut off from it when the river made a turn west. The smaller group would be dealt with later after the immediate threat was eliminated.

The raid further reduced the threat of MA to about 800,000, the thinning optimizer reported. If Lambeau could bring to bear enough assets against MA, the refugee camp had a chance of surviving.

"If Lambeau is throwing everything it has at defending themselves, what is left for us?" Ruth Ann observed.

I knew the answer but didn't voice it out loud. I raised my estimate of how many of CB2 would arrive on my lawn.

Bill said, "I don't see why they would expend many resources on CB2 when it's marching over ground that's already been trampled. There is very little chance there is anything our way worth saving except us."

"We ought to talk about strategy Bill for your men when CB2 gets here," I said. "There is no way your weapons will keep them off of us. If your men do fire it would draw more towards us even the fuel cell seems to be."

"I told you Doug. These second floor windows will be the first thing to give out. If they start climbing over each other, they will pour in here like ants on a picnic lunch."

"Lovely analogy, Bill. Thank you for that," Ruth Ann added.

"When CBA gets close we have to shut off the fuel cell whether Lambeau likes it not. Our lives depend on it. When that happens, Bill, are you prepared to say no if Lambeau orders you to keep our systems running?"

"Doug, I won't answer that. I am a soldier. If given a lawful order I have to obey it."

"You're human too. Hell you are practically my insurance man. Our life insurance plans with the same company as the house. You cause us to get killed your company is going to be out millions."

"Actually that's not quite right Doug. Our policies have exceptions for acts of God and war. Let's hope it doesn't come to that, OK?

"You are not being very comforting right now Bill."

◆ CB2 was north of Tomah already.

At the fork where I-90 and I-94 split, with I-90 heading due west, Lambeau tried something new and cheap to divert some undead from continuing on I-94 towards us.

Three Blackhawks suspended a man each just above and just out of reach of the face of the advancing horde. Armed only with bullhorns and guns they tried to get the zombie's attention. They were to play the part of the Pied Piper in trying to steer rats into the forests and rough terrain near and past Fort McCoy.

The bluffs overlooking the I-90, as it got closer to the Mississippi, were perfect for squad-sized teams to lay in ambush with mortars. Firing mortars would not make loud enough noise for the dead to localize. Lambeau hoped to cut the number of dead down with a "death of a thousand cuts" if you pardon the expression. If the dead vectored in on a squad, it could melt into the landscape.

The bridges over the Mississippi at French Island in La Crosse were the most significant bridges in the Midwest Administrative Zone to have been destroyed so far. French Island still functioned as a refuge. With no bridges connecting to it, the Mighty Mississippi kept French Island safe.

It was forty-two miles from the fork of the interstates to French Island. Lambeau expected that the number of dead killed off along the route would be sufficient so that the remainder would not pose a significant threat to the refuge. Just the same, ground troops were ferried into the airport there from Camp Ripley, the winter warfare training center in Minnesota.

With my high-resolution satellite feed we could watch the progress of the diversion attempt. Again, I connected the images to our big screen TV. This entertainment, updated each minute, provided important relief to the tension of the long wait for CB2.

"Check it out, the helicopters are hovering right over the fork!" a soldier named Chris Evans said.

"I bet they start moving to the west, they want to draw Zekes onto 90," said Sgt. Orderly.

Appearing suddenly, a string of white smoke billowed over the area north of the interchange, where I-94 continued northwest.

"What's that about? Napalm?" said Evans.

"No, there are no flames. We would see them even in daylight. No. They're trying to cover up 94 like closing a curtain so more will follow on 90."

Orderly was right. The three helicopters began creeping west almost indiscernibly slowly. It took several minute-by-minute updates to tell for sure. More smoke continued to billow up over the I-94 portion of the highway.

"I don't see any helicopters near there. Where is the smoke coming from?" I asked.

"Probably from howitzers at Fort McCoy. They can fire up to eleven miles. McCoy is a little further away than that but the howitzers move," Orderly said.

Bill was watching too. He added, "There were self-propelled howitzers there for training when this all started. The smoke is probably courtesy of them."

Fort McCoy was a substantial training base for the U.S. Army. Every time I drove past there I knew there was more to the place than some dusty barrack like buildings visible from the highway.

"You know they're a lot closer to us than they are to Door County. Maybe they can help us when CB2 gets here. Lieutenant, would you be willing to run that up the chain?"

"I can do that Mr. Handsman. If those are self-propelled guns they could be here in under four hours without traffic. Ten or twelve at the most."

Thank goodness for small favors.

Just imagine those men swinging from lines shouting through megaphones and waving just out of reach of more than three million zombies. I don't know if they were in baskets or harnesses but they must have been freezing and frightened. Yet, they were there doing what they were ordered to do. One wrong twitch by the helicopter's pilots and you know they would have been cut loose by the crew chief up above rather than risk having the chopper be exposed to a clawed, bitten, or even mauled comrade.

The technique was working.

As the helicopters crept west a finger of undead followed them. The finger widened and deepened. After half an hour of updates, I made an estimate of the number of undead drawn off the path towards us based upon the size of the contour surrounding them. Incredibly, I estimated 200,000 ghouls.

"They better stop. That's too many to kill before they get to La Cross," I said.

Each zombie taken off the northwest path would be one less we would see here. Still, we are only thirteen people. There were hundreds on French Island. The Doug Handsman I grew up with wouldn't care about those people. Not a whit. The person who spoke last could not possibly be me. But it was.

In the next minute's update, smoke appeared at the rear of the mass heading west visually cutting them off from the main body moving northwest. Smoke rounds continued to burst near the westward divergence of I-90 while the area over I-94 was allowed to clear. They used the smoke like valves to shunt a group of undead to the west. Then, when they switched the smoke's location, it was like closing the valve leading west and opening the one leading north. Soon a gap appeared between the rear edge of the group that had broken off and the main horde. Amazingly, this attempt at steering was successful.

For the price of several hours' use of three helicopters, some unbelievably brave men and smoke rounds, a significant body of walking dead was split off from their horde. This effort would serve as a model for other attempts around the country.

◆ I showed Ruth Ann some of the fruit of my labors here at Christmas Tree. A few of the virtual web hosts, those make believe computers I had set up, were filling with data about missing persons, mostly children. Tens of thousands of photographs of kids along with identifying information were being uploaded by Lambeau, more every minute.

I didn't fully appreciate why it was important for me to set up web hosting on my servers when there were zombies to find and kill. However, after looking at the photographs I counted helping to reconnect parents and children as among Christmas Tree's most important functions.

Around 3 PM, Bill came over to talk.

"Brandt just told me about another aerial mining mission north of Port Washington."

"Really, I didn't see that kicked out by the optimizer."

"Yeah, this one was ordered the old fashioned way. It shows you how on edge they are."

"They were supposed to be having down time today for repairs."

"There is a lot at stake. Let me run an idea by you."

"Shoot."

"What about taking down the garage door ourselves and using the material to board up the second floor windows?"

"OK. That sounds *so* irrational you must have a good reason for thinking it'll help."

"If Zeke gets into the second floor, we're lost. There is no separation between the first and second floors. Giving them access to the garage means access to a small doorway that we can shore up. We'd leave your car in there and move the 4x4 back in. There wouldn't be enough room for the Zekes to mass."

"We're using the back door out of the garage as our main door. If we open the garage to the outside and board up the inner door how will we get in and out of house?"

"We saw you have some rope ladders in case of fire. We can use those hooked up at the roof."

"OK. Now you *are* irrational. Look at me. I am more than one cannoli past my prime. I bought those things out of habit, not because I ever thought I would or could use them. If we do as you are saying, I will be a shut-in."

Of course, I was already for all intents and purposes.

"OK. I'll keep thinking about it."

"How about the cars? If we take the wheels off the cars we have, Ryan's, and mine we can position them in front of but away from the building. As obstacles. No. That's a stupid idea. Yeah, you keep thinking about it."

I thought for a moment myself and continued, "Actually, all this talk about shutting me in makes me want to go for a walk. Can you hook me up with an escort?"

"Sure, I'll go with you."

No sooner did the two of us plus two soldiers, Specialists Bob Peretz and Bob Wisnewski – Bob and Bob, get outside than a thought occurred to me.

"What about the home supply distribution warehouse east of us?"

"Doh!" exclaimed Bill. "When we operated the safe zone we raided it a bunch of times. There should still be things there we could use."

"Sometimes it takes some fresh air to get fresh ideas."

"Puh," said Specialist Bob's rifle.

"Puh. Puh." said the other Specialist Bob's weapon.

"Why don't we make this a short walk?" I said.

"Yeah, sounds like a good idea."

"Puh."

◆ Over the Monday night and into Tuesday (Day 41), mortar teams attacked the small horde splintered off of CB2 along the path towards La Crosse and French Island. In the dark, and set back by as much as two kilometers, not a single team had been challenged. These efforts were remarkably efficient.

Just the same, a flight of three Blackhawks were spared from Lambeau Field and relocated to French Island along with resupplies of fuel and weapons for both the mortar teams and the helicopters.

The mortar teams and choppers made steady progress throughout the day. The consensus was that French Island would remain safe given continued attacks against the dead.

My morning meeting with Frank produced little good will and even less results.

"How's it going there Frank, all rested, repaired and resupplied?"

"We have made good use of the lull Walter. Before you ask, the answer is no. Nothing has changed with regard to evacuating you."

"Come on. I made a strong argument for staying here but as you military people say, conditions on the ground have changed. How could I know we would have to sit through a second horde even bigger than the first?"

"We cannot do without your data center's results."

"But you can *do* just fine with the data center's destruction? That doesn't make sense Frank."

"We don't believe you are in danger of being overrun if you maintain stealth."

"Stealth doesn't seem possible anymore. The fuel cell system is definitely attracting Zeke. Have your people figured out what is drawing them?"

"We have not made progress on that, no."

"You can see our cameras. They congregate at the fuel cell fence. Sometimes they get agitated and bang on it before we put them down. I don't see how we can survive a horde banging away like that. Before CB2 gets here, we have to shut down. You see that right?"

"At this time shutting down is not an option."

"Oh come on. Seriously? You must have some computers in all of Door County. My people there can cobble together a temporary data center. We can run in both places at the same time for a clean hand-off. We have almost two days to get this done."

"We search every building we clear, Walter. You know tourism was the main industry in Door County before all this. The best we have come up with is old equipment from lawyers and doctors offices. Your data center is the only game in town."

"What about the supercomputer company in Chippewa Falls? There must be something there we can use."

"The buildings did not survive. I wanted to avoid saying this, but if we didn't have to put up with your prima donna antics, we wouldn't. I said your data center is the only game in town. If we had other options, we would be using them. Is that clear enough for you?"

Ouch.

"What if I just switch the whole thing off?"

"The officer at your location will hold a gun to your head until you turn it back on."

"And if I refuse?"

"The officer will pull his trigger and the technical specialist will turn the computers back on."

"You would throw away my skills just like that? In the whole country there are probably only a thousand people with my combination of skills and experience."

"Suppose that's true Walter. You are a numbers man, let's do the math. From approximately 300,000,000 Americans you say you are one in a thousand. So for every 300,000 people on average there is one of you. We have 300,000 people in

Lambeau Field and you are the precious genius we drew. Are you with me so far?"

I did not like where this was going.

"Across the Administrative Zones we are collecting more survivors every day. Soon the probability of finding another computer czar is going to pay off. Besides, there are people here including myself who think you're not the rock star you think you are."

I was silent. The problem with having a worldview of "people suck," is that after a while people notice. Back in Silicon Valley it didn't matter because I wielded real power and, my world view was the rule, not the exception. Recently I found myself growing to appreciate being part of the human race more and more but it is too late. I was typecast.

Frank came back with an olive branch: "Look, you have been working with us only for a few days. In that short time, you have accomplished great things with the optimizer and web servers. You have come up with solutions to big problems you weren't asked about. Play ball with us Walter. Sit tight, we will do our best to keep you safe. I have to go, Lambeau Field out."

Bill Mancheski heard the entire exchange. I turned to him and said, "You wouldn't shoot me would you?"

"It would make me very sad to shoot you."

"Thanks buddy."

◆ CB2 passed Black River Falls. Lambeau had ordered no further attacks on the horde. Except for the possibility that one or two zombies might have fallen down and broken a leg, the size of the horde was unchanged.

The horde bearing down on Door County was south of Manitowoc. Manitowoc had a rich maritime history and played an important part in trade on the Great Lakes. It lay just 30 miles south of where the defensive line for Door County was intended to be along Highway 29.

Military commanders made a wise decision to stop their advance towards Highway 29 and build a stronger defense starting north of Kewaunee to take advantage of the Kewaunee River. Meandering northwest, the actual defensive line was about 8 miles further north of Highway 29 giving four hours more to dig in.

Stopping further north than anticipated also meant the military would not have to contend with the eastern half of Green Bay. Not having to deal right now with Green Bay, by far the largest city in the area was a major plus.

One other benefit of stopping to the north was that Interstate 43, the path that MA was following, sloped away to the northwest just as it approached Door County. If the horde stuck to the highway, there was a chance Lambeau could be spared entirely. If the line had been built at Highway 29, it would have crossed the Interstate, directly exposing Lambeau's position to the horde.

Two massive operations were planned for today. A two-mile wide area south of Manitowoc would be mined in depth. The horde would hit the minefield just after noon.

We watched fixed wing and rotary aircraft crisscross over the area about to become an impassible no man's land. Learning from the previous use of aerial mines, this time the mines were laid in an inverted V, sort of bell curve shaped, pattern. Last time, mines had been placed in a rectangular box. Most of the mines to the sides went unused as the horde narrowed in behind a spearhead. By shaping the minefield in an inverted V the mission planners counted on shifting the horde in a planned way, rather than the unexpected way the horde did on its own last time.

The horde hit the minefield in an ovular blob and immediately shaped into the planned narrowing point. In the daylight, the crowd that gathered around our big screen TV couldn't see many flashes as individual mines detonated. It would be an hour before we would see pockmarks and bodies strewn about.

However, before the hour had elapsed, the crowd in front of the television had departed on a mission to liberate building supplies from a warehouse to our east.

Of the eleven soldiers stationed at Camp Christmas Tree five remained behind. Four continued the watch on the roof and one to operate the radio. Lieutenant Mancheski took both of our vehicles, our Volvo station wagon and Ryan's 4x4, the other five soldiers plus Ruth Ann on the mission.

Ruth Ann had all but begged to go. Her credentials as a sniper earned her a place in the 4x4. With its roof removed it resembled an old fashioned Jeep. She gave her word she would remain in the vehicle and provide cover for the advance and return of the assault team. Specialist Bob Wisnewski would also remain in the 4x4 to cover Ruth Ann and to act as a driver in case the idling vehicle was in danger of being overrun.

Before leaving, the 4x4 was topped off with gas from the five-gallon can Ruth Ann had purchased before everything stopped and the people fled. The Volvo still had nearly a full tank. With the added five gallons in the 4x4 both vehicles had plenty of fuel to make what in theory was an eight-mile roundtrip.

Ruth Ann and I said our goodbyes.

"Don't worry about me Doug. I'm sure the guys will take care of me."

"I'm sure they will hon. I'm sure you'll do great against a few dead. What if you find yourselves surrounded by too many Zekes for seven people to handle? You know they win with overwhelming numbers."

"While you were watching MA hit the minefield we were watching a close up of the warehouse. There aren't too many creatures there."

"Based on movement? You wouldn't be able to spot the statues even with our highest resolution pictures. Also, you can't see inside the buildings. You guys don't actually know what you're heading into."

"Hon, if it's bad we'll turn around. Besides look at this shiny new gun they gave me. I just *have* to try it out," Ruth Ann said this in a joking way like she was talking about strutting in new shoes. She raised a sound suppressed weapon that was larger and heavier than the assault rifles I had seen before.

"Wow," I looked at it. "Is it a boy or girl?"

Ruth Ann smiled and lowered the weapon to her side. She leaned in to give me a kiss. I leaned into her just a bit harder than called for and surrounded my kiss with a hug.

Our watch on the roof put down the walking dead in our immediate area. From farther away the dead continued to be drawn towards the fuel cell system like dogs to a hydrant, always the same spot.

While the men on the roof kept watch, the departing team raised the garage door and warmed up the vehicles to make sure they were in running order. When they left I reengaged only one of the door's hasps and locked the inner door.

"Base this is six. Radio check."

"Six this is base. Five by five. Good luck."

I had programming to work on so I plugged in a laptop within earshot of the radio. My work for the day was to begin writing a system to help identify people, children mostly, from pictures. Unlike my previous tasks, this one could take a lot of time.

I have already described the first big website that went live on my servers. It was a site to help survivors find other survivors. Mostly, it was for parents to find lost children. As pictures were entered, certain basic information such as gender, age and hair color was entered as well. Of course, names, birthdays and even social security numbers would narrow a search down instantly to a single or small number of individuals. Nevertheless, all the identifiers we use in our modern age of information were useless if the person was too young or too traumatized to communicate.

For these people, facial recognition would be required. This is a not a straightforward task.

I was just finishing making myself comfortable when the radio came to life.

"Six to base."

"Go ahead six."

"Pass on to Lambeau we can see Zeke headed in your direction from at least half a mile away. Whatever is bringing them in; it carries at least that far."

"Copy Six. Half mile. Will pass it on."

Great. When the crush of CB2 is upon us, we'll be a bright light to the moths. I was still thinking about this last bit of news when the radio came alive again.

"Six to base."

"Go ahead six."

"Highway Twelve and Vollendorf Lane. Engaging eight Zekes."

"Copy."

"Zeke is down. Count twelve more visible in the next klick. Proceeding."

"Copy that. Dozen Zekes over the next kilometer."

I wasn't going to get anything done. At this point I started doodling boxes in three point perspective and coloring in their sides.

"Christmas Tree this is Six. Big rig blocking Chuck Lane east bound. Going around. We're switching to play by play."

"Copy Six. Play by play."

I looked at Brandt and asked what "play by play" was.

"They are close to the warehouse and will be talking to each other now."

"We will be able to hear them?"

"Yes. That's what the Lieutenant means by play by play."

We listened in.

"Fences look good from here. Chuck, go north to the truck entrance. Take a look. We'll stay here to cover you."

A mike clicked.

A moment later, "LT, the truck entrance doesn't have a rigid gate. Just barriers. Zeke can walk in and out if they want."

"Copy. Come on back. Let's take a look at the rest of the fencing. The plywood we want is further to the east."

A moment passed.

"Movement in the office windows," came Bill Mancheski's voice.

"Walkers near the fences, LT."

"Copy that. They have eyes on us. Take them out. We don't need them following us into the campus."

"Hooah."

A moment passed.

"Barry, we're turning left into this entrance. Swing ahead of us to raise the barriers. We have your back."

"Copy LT."

"And go through the guard's hut. See if they have a directory of the warehouses. I know where the plywood is but we need adhesive too. No idea where we will find that."

Ruth Ann told me later that one of Bill's men, Specialist John Rentmiesters, clipped chains on both barriers and left them raised. They wouldn't keep out walkers but they would impede a hasty exit by our vehicles.

"Gates up. I can see stacks of plywood ahead to the right," said John's voice.

"Is there a directory in the guard shack?"

"Looking now."

"Barry, two Zekes approaching. You have eyes on them?"

Specialist Barry Clark was standing watch next to the Volvo. Two zombies were staggering towards him.

"I got them, boss… two Zekes down. I don't see any others."

"There's one coming out from behind the wall at the parking lot to the west. We'll take it."

"Six," John's voice, "good news, we scored a directory. Warehouse three has construction adhesives and caulk. Bad news, that warehouse is at the west end of the compound."

The group had made their entrance at the far eastern end of the complex.

"Copy. Load up on plywood. We'll provide cover."

Later Ruth Ann filled in some of the details that didn't go out over the radio.

"Bill is a smart young man. A planner and a worrier in his own way just like you. Even though the plywood was right there he had us pull around the stacks so that we were as hidden as we could be from the gates and still pointed towards them. If we had to bug out, we didn't need to turn around."

She continued, "Then he told everyone under no circumstances should we engage any dead at or near the gates. We had to keep the path through the gates clear of bodies. At each step he was thinking about the next and also how to keep escape routes open. It was neat watching him command knowing a few weeks ago he was an insurance salesman."

"The men loaded twelve sheets of plywood into the Volvo. Bill called a huddle with Bob, our driver and Barry who was driving the Volvo," she said.

"We are here," said Bill pointing to the east end of map in the campus directory. "Warehouse three is here," pointing to the west end of the campus. "As you can see there is no straight path between here and there. Plus, all the routes between here and there are narrow. Perfect for getting surrounded."

As Bill pointed out, an enormous warehouse stretched north south all but blocking passage east west. To get around the building to the south would mean a thousand feet of narrow passage with one side bounded by loading bays hiding who knew what. To get around the building to the north would mean an even longer path with three blind turns and loading bays on both two sides.

He continued, "We're going to exit the way we came in, turn west and head to the next set of gates. We'll make our entry there and the warehouse will be straight ahead.

On my laptop, I could see the road along the southern wall of the warehouse campus was changing color. There were dead on the move.

"Brandt tell them the dead are moving in behind them. Look at my laptop."

"Six this is Christmas Tree. Six this is Christmas Tree."

"Six, go ahead."

"Satellite shows dead are walking on the main road. We can't tell which direction based on our latest picture and we can't tell exactly how many, sir."

"When is your next picture Christmas Tree?"

"Almost a minute from now sir. A lot can change in a minute."

"Understood Christmas Tree, keep us advised. Six out."

Back on the radio I heard, "Everybody set? We have to boogey."

A mike click came back.

“OK. We’re turning west folks. Move out.”

The gates they were passing through were set two hundred feet in from the main road. Their view of the main road would be blocked to the west by a wall until they reached the road itself.

“LT the way is blocked. I say again, the way is blocked.”

A moment later, “I see them Barry. I make about two hundred hostiles heading towards us. Barry?”

“Affirmative LT. More coming behind them from the office buildings down the street.”

True enough. Had our people stayed inside much longer the gates they had entered would have choked with the dead.

“Six, this is Christmas Tree. Confirm estimate of two hundred on the road in your direction. Estimate two hundred more converging on your area.”

Bill had to make a split second decision.

“Lim, hop out and get in our car. We are going back into the complex. Barry, you back up due east to the intersection with Kane Road. Make sure you draw them with you. Don’t let any go in the gates after us. Once you get to Kane Road hold their interest as long as you can and then escape either north or south. It doesn’t matter, you know the way back to Christmas Tree after that. Understood?”

“Hooah.”

Specialist Lim Zsu ran between the cars. In my nervousness I asked Brandt, “How come everyone is a Specialist? Who washes dishes?”

Brandt shrugged. “The guys who wash dishes are Specialists too. It’s like clerks being Customer Service Consultants, it’s good for our self-esteem.”

Then it hit me. Bill’s car was going back inside the compound. As the dead headed east outside the wall towards Barry’s diversion, Bill was going to head west on the other side of the wall. Bill's team would be entering warehouse three by themselves.

Ruth Ann was in Bill's team.

Bill's voice, "We are clear of the gates Barry. Make them chase you. Good luck and see you back at camp."

"Copy LT. The dead are almost to the street leading to your gates. We are engaging and falling back slowly. We have their full attention."

The sound of automatic weapons wire almost drowned out Barry Clark's voice.

About a minute passed.

"LT we kept them under fire as long as we could. There are still more coming. We haven't seen any break off to follow you through the gates. Who knows what they will do after we bug out. We are heading south to Highway 12 and back to the Tree. Good luck sir."

Bill clicked his mike in acknowledgment.

"Six this is Christmas Tree."

"Go ahead."

"Our latest picture shows you have passed the main body. They are pooling at Kane and the main road. We see no movement into the compound. I say again, no movement into the compound."

"Understood."

Ruth Ann continued the story from here:

"As we passed west along the wall we didn't see any zombies ahead of us. But Lim saw some coming out from behind tractor trailers behind us. Apparently we were going fast enough to be past them before they noticed."

She continued, "As we got closer to the turn we saw three statues in the far corner. They noticed us and perked up. Bill said we would have to drop them because being so close to the road, their noises might be heard on the other side."

"Bill stood on the passenger seat and I stood in the rear. We took out all three as we approached. It was so cool Doug you should have been there."

I gave my wife a fake half smile.

"When we made the turn slowly towards warehouse three there was another small group coming towards the commotion. Lim, Bill and I dropped them immediately."

"These definitely weren't workers from nearby. The ghouls had been all sorts of people. These were leftovers from the Twin Cities horde that passed through here. A lot of them were really far gone. Maybe that is why they were still in the compound. That, and there were so many twisty little turns and places to get lost in. By then I was convinced going inside a building was a bad idea."

"Bob made the sharp left slowly. As soon as we saw the full area we saw just how big warehouse three was, plus a few more walkers."

"Bill ordered Bob to stop at the gates first. While we, Bill and I, shot the ghouls we could see, Lim hopped out a shot the locks off the gates and raised them for our escape route. We could see a dribble of ghouls walking on the main road still headed east to Kane where the crowd was milling."

"I was looking at the few walkers passing by and Lim must have been too because a ghoul crashed through the glass of the guard hut. Just shattered it. I saw it an instant before it came through the glass and was already yelling to Lim. The zombie fell out of the guard hut. Lim had a chance to swing his weapon around to nail the gate crasher through the back of its head."

"That was close," Lim said.

"Bill told Bob to head over to the warehouse and to turn around facing the exit like we did before. Bob did that. When we stopped, Bill said we had come a long way to give up without a look inside. He said,"

"Lim, you're with me. It isn't ideal to go in there with just you but Bob, you have to stay here with Mrs. Handsman. One person can't stay out here alone. Lim, we're looking for anything that will hold the plywood in place. Liquid Nails preferably. Failing that look for masonry bits and screws. Ruth Ann, do you have a drill? Something heavy duty? Not cordless. Extension cords?"

"Yeah, we have plenty of cords and a drill."

"OK. Stay in touch by radio. Bob, you've got Mrs. Handsman. Lim you're on me. Let's go."

Lieutenant Mancheski and Specialist Zsu disappeared into the dimness of a series of covered loading bays. Inside they saw one bay whose giant door was rolled up, easy access for them into the warehouse and of course, the undead as well. Once inside the sunlight streamed in from translucent panels making up the warehouse roof. Seeing the cavernous interior well lit, the two soldiers felt a lift in their spirits.

That lift was immediately countered when they saw how many aisles there were.

"There must be thousands of different products in here. It wouldn't be the first time I left one of this company's stores without finding what I needed," Bill whispered.

"I'm not from around here LT. We don't have these where I'm from."

The two stopped, back to back against the wall near the door they entered. Silently they scanned for threats while listening for any noise. There were irregular scraping noises and moaning come from inside the warehouse. There were a number of forklifts and pallet trucks nearby.

Quietly Lim said, "LT, on the forklifts. Clipboards. Maybe they're pick lists that tell the operators what to get and where to get it."

Lt. Mancheski signaled his approval at Lim's observation and motioned to the closest forklift. They crept quickly to the machine. They knelt back to back for a moment, listening. One of the moans was a bit louder. Lim grabbed the clipboard. It was a pick list but contained nothing useful.

They had many more forklifts to look at. This area closest to the loading bays contained twenty-two aisles and was the narrowest part of the building. The next forklift turned up nothing useful and neither did the next. One moan kept getting louder.

Looking at the fourth forklift they could see it was slightly off kilter. It seemed to sit with its far corner raised slightly. The moaning was definitely coming from that machine. Bill touched Lim to get his attention. He removed his fixed blade combat knife from its sheath and motioned to himself. Lim readied to cover his Lieutenant.

As they got closer to the forklift, they readily saw why it was canted. One wheel rested squarely on a zombie's low back. It clawed at the ground with its outstretched left arm. Its right arm was motionless, squashed nearly flat by the forklift. It looked as though the heavy back end had ridden up the length of the ghoul's right arm, over its spine coming to rest near its buttocks. The thing became aware of Bill as he got close. Its head snapped from looking right towards the forklift to left to howl at Bill. Bill's combat knife entered the creature's skull just behind its ear and sliced downward towards its brain stem. It went silent and limp.

As Bill rose, withdrawing his knife, he saw a clipboard on the floor of the cockpit. Looking through it, he found nothing of help. "Oh for four," he thought to himself. As he turned to signal Lim something caught his eye. A thick dog-eared flipbook was attached to the machine's safety cage in reach of the missing driver's right hand. Bill cut the zip tie that held the flipbook to the cage. Thumbing through it, it was immediately clear it was a complete catalog of the warehouse. He handed the flipbook to Lim and used disinfectant swabs to clean his knife.

Lim said, “Concrete fasteners, aisle 71.”

“This is Six. We have located a warehouse manifest. We’ll be heading deeper into the building. Bob, say your state.”

Bob’s voice returned, “We are in light but steady contact, over.”

“And our guest?”

“Our guest is doing fine. She would make an excellent sniper LT. Can we keep her?”

I breathed in deeply for the first time since Ruth Ann’s vehicle went back into the compound alone.

“That’s a discussion for another day, Bob. Christmas Tree, say updates.”

“Six this is Christmas Tree. Last pictures show the crowd spreading out. There are walkers at the east entrance heading inside. Over.”

“Understood. Say update on Mike Alpha?”

“Milwaukee A is deep into the minefield sir. Mr. Christmas Tree says he can’t tell yet how effective it has been. Over.”

Off radio, Bill whispered “Ready? Aisle 71. Down this aisle, we’ll see where it leaves us.”

As the two walked, Bill covering ahead of them, Lim covering behind them, scraping sounds, and more moaning became louder. They reached the next intersection to find themselves across from aisle 40, construction shoes. They stopped to listen. Lim sipped water from his camel back. They heard a soft tapping from the west. Bill peered around the corner in that direction. A zombie stood five aisles down slowly rocking from foot to foot but was otherwise quiescent.

Bill motioned to Lim one threat. Bill knelt by the corner and readied his sound suppressed rifle. Leaning forward he took aim and fired. As he did so, the zombie saw the movement and bellowed. Bill’s shot took the ghoul out cleanly. But not without cost. From behind both sides of the aisle five rows down came sounds of movement and moaning. With Lim at Bill's back covering their flank and rear Bill readied for more contacts.

A walker missing the left side of its face and burns down its left side appeared followed by another Zeke.

"Puh. Puh," spoke Bill. He tapped behind for Lim's attention and motioned to move out. They made their way down aisle 40 quickly. Noise in the building was picking up.

In their earpieces they heard Bob Wisnewski, "LT, contact is ticking up. We're still good. Hope you're back soon." Bill clicked his mike in acknowledgment.

Arriving at the next intersection, they found themselves looking at aisle 81. Now they needed to go west, still further away from the door they had entered.

"Bob, Six. When we get to what we need we will be at the northwest part of the building. Can you relocate there?"

"Affirmative. On the move."

Bob turned to Ruth Ann and said, "Hold on, we're moving closer to the LT for pickup. Hold on and keep firing. Take my weapon. It's lighter."

Ruth Ann put her longer-range rifle down to take Bob's assault rifle. Bob withdrew is sidearm and placed it in his lap as he began to drive the car west. Ruth Ann engaged the walkers in their path.

Bill and Lim finally arrived at the promised aisle with no further contact but noises were still getting closer. Each taking a side of the aisle, they scanned for what they needed.

Lim found a pallet of long masonry screws. The two paused while Lim used his combat knife to slice open the shrink-wrap surrounding the pallet. He grabbed on case and looked to his Lieutenant. Bill whispered, "I doubt they have masonry bits for their drill. Let's keep looking for the glue."

Fifteen feet further down the aisle, they found a pallet of Liquid Nails. Bill repeated the steps Lim had taken to extract two cases of the product. He handed one case to Lim who put down the case of masonry screws and reloaded his weapon. Each holding a case, zombies appeared at both ends of aisle 71.

"LT. In position. Be advised it is a tight space and we are in contact."

On their way out now, Bill was less concerned with stealth. Without whispering, "Lim, fire at will. Head north then turn left."

Lim began quickly firing double taps to make sure the ghouls ahead of them went down permanently. Bill did the same with those behind them.

"Reloading," Bill shouted as they kept moving for the doors on the west side of the building. When they reached the doors, they found none open. Rather than trying the doors, Bill pulled a grenade from his vest.

"Bob, are you clear of door 3 Golf? I'm going to make a hole."

"Affirmative."

"Fire in the hole," Bill yelled as he tossed the grenade at the wall. Lim continued to firing as they both ducked behind cases of BBQ potato chips. Bill had time to say, "Don't ever tell anyone we used potato chips for cover."

The grenade blew door 3G open letting sweet sunlight pour through the opening. Bill and Lim were on the move.

They ran across the railroad tracks to find Bob and Ruth Ann waiting. Bob had already turned the vehicle around to head towards the exit. Ruth Ann was firing methodically. Bill and Lim tossed their finds into the rear of the car and hopped in. Bill shouted, "GO!"

Bob accelerated in the direction they had come. Both Lim and Ruth Ann fired forward. Bill watched their flank and rear. As they rounded a corner, a zombie appeared right at Bob's side. With a quick motion, Bob raised his 9mm and completely opened the skull of the ghoul. Almost to the exit, Ruth Ann, Lim and Bill fired forward. There were many zombies in the area now.

Unavoidably Bob had to run over several bodies causing his passengers to hold on for dear life. Several zombies nearly reached the open sides of the 4x4. Bob couldn't spare a hand to use his sidearm. A ragged claw grabbed a tenuous hold on Bob's uniformed shoulder. Bill drilled it with two rounds, the first splitting the ghouls arm in two the next nailing it in the head as it fell behind. The claw hung on to Bob's uniform for a moment before falling off.

As they turned right with the exit immediately before them, they had no choice but to ram the zombies blocking the lanes ahead. Through the gate, the three shooters resumed firing. Thankfully, the short street to the main road was only lightly filled.

Ruth Ann shouted, "I'm out. Give me another weapon." Now was not the time to learn the proper technique for reloading an assault rifle. Bill exchanged rifles with Ruth Ann and reloaded what had been hers during the short lull.

Turning right again onto the main road they saw behind them a boiling mass of hundreds of undead too far back to be a threat. Ahead of them were only a few, easy pickings for the three expert shots.

Soon, they were on Highway 12 heading home. Moving quickly they needed to de-animate only a few undead.

They arrived at Christmas Tree barely an hour after leaving.

◆ When they returned they were greeted by myself, Barry Clark and John Rentmiesters both of whom had come back in the Volvo with a dozen sheets of plywood.

I all but lunged at Ruth Ann and gave her a bear hug. She gave me a brilliant smile and said, "It's nice to be home. Let me clean up and I'll make some lunch."

My wife went from zombie sniper to Betty Crocker in a heartbeat. I was still standing there with my jaw hanging down when Bill said, "You heard her, lunch!"

We ate watching the big screen results of the mining south of Manitowoc. The size of the contour leaving the minefield was considerably smaller than the one that went it. Behind the advancing, now smaller horde, was a mass of slowly writhing pixels. I estimated the MA horde at just 600,000 left. Just 600,000 zombies! It was shaping up to be a good day in Lambeau Field.

The group left behind at the bend in the Milwaukee River seemed to like it there. They weren't moving much.

The band heading west towards French Island continued to oblige by making themselves great targets for mortars and gunships.

Everybody was having a great day.

◆ As far as I could tell, CB2 hadn't suffered a single casualty. It was getting closer by the minute.

Before lunch Brandt read the directions on the Liquid Nails and brought the cases inside to warm up. Apparently the goo is more effective if it isn't cold.

Bill and I checked in with Frank. Bill explained his successful raid on the home supply distribution center. He mentioned the grace exhibited in battle by his team especially Mrs. Christmas Tree.

"You took her with you?"

"Affirmative sir. She was amazing."

"Well, I glad it worked out. I have enough problems with Walter as it is. I don't want to think about how difficult he would be if Mrs. Christmas Tree didn't come back."

"I'm standing right here you know, Frank," I said.

"Yes, Walter, I know that. I said what I said specifically for your benefit."

"That's enough. Man to faceless voice on the radio I'm tired of the shit you're giving me. My wife and I are working our asses off and making a difference. Even if you're not telling me, I can see the number of children we've put back with their parents around the country and my guys tell me the automatic rifles and Claymores I made for you are saving lives. I'll take responsibility for being a prima donna before but I think I've earned some slack from you. And if I keep arguing to be evacuated you can't blame me for wanting *all* the people here to live through CB2."

"Are you finished?"

"Yes."

"Then you will be pleased to know we are making arrangements with the North Western Administrative Zone to shift assets our way. Many people are trying very hard to keep *all* of us alive, including Christmas Tree. You have to keep your computers running. We're hooked up to all the Administrative

Zones now. Your data center is handling analysis for the entire country and Puerto Rico too. You have to keep your computers running. Agreed?"

That made me feel a lot better.

"Agreed."

"Good. One last thing, have you been backing up your systems right?"

"Of course, why?"

"Send us a copy, will you?"

That made me feel a lot less confident.

"Sure thing Frank."

"Good. Lambeau out."

I did not intend to send Lambeau the backup. If they had it, there would be one less reason for rescue.

◆ Starting with the windows overlooking the fuel cell system, the men took down the shutters, slathered adhesive on both the concrete and wood, and held the wood in place while the goo set. The first attempt was a fail, perhaps due to the cold weather. The second and subsequent attempts succeeded by holding the wood in place for a much longer time. Two soldiers at a time balanced on our ladder to accomplish this.

Brandt said the rated curing time for the adhesive was seven days. We would have two days, but it would be better than none.

◆ About 8 PM, those off duty gathered around the TV again to watch the day's second strike against MA unfold. The nature of the strike was somewhat of a surprise to me. A squadron of B-52s from North Dakota was to bring their unique form of thunder down on Milwaukee A.

From our seats on an orbiting satellite, this one was really something.

Milwaukee A was now north of Manitowoc near the Maribel Caves. The absence of favorable terrain was irrelevant in face of the density of the bombing. High explosives fell in a deluge causing an area of solid intense glowing in the infrared stream. In normal color, the explosions glowed equally brightly. So brightly, in fact, that the shockwave of each successive explosion was visible in the light of the last.

The massive pounding continued for only a few minutes. The targets, being soft, slow and exposed didn't necessitate going longer.

In morning's light helicopters would take a close look at the results.

Before Ruth Ann and I turned in, I checked on what was happening down in the datacenter. I opened the door to the machine room to find Brandt inspecting the equipment. I was sure he looked like a person who had hurriedly gone into a "Who me?" pose. My hunch was confirmed when he turned towards me with his right hand unnaturally buried in his pants pocket. When his hand reemerged, Brandt had a bulge in his pants. I am certain it wasn't there because he was happy to see me.

"Ah, Specialist. What brings you down to my toy room?" I said without letting on about my suspicions.

"I'm just admiring your set up sir. I still can't believe this small room in a concrete house is the biggest datacenter in the Midwest."

"It isn't the biggest Specialist. It is the most convenient. There are huge datacenters in the cities that make this look like the closet it is. But that's just it. They are huge. It would take a lot more than a fuel cell to keep them cool and powered up. You know I heard a talk once from somebody at one of the big search providers. The guy said that by 2050, half of the electricity in the United States would be used by datacenters."

"That much?"

"Yeah, and that's just the U.S. Well good night, Specialist. I'll close the door behind you." I said this with my arm outstretched in an obvious gesture to have him leave.

"Uh, good night Mr. Handsman."

I closed the door behind Brandt and gave my equipment a quick but thorough looking over. I didn't expect to see any new boxes with blinking red lights wired into my rig. Whatever it was that Brandt was doing would be invisible to the eye. Physical access to a machine is the surest way to have malware deployed on your system. Brandt had had such access for who knows how long or how many times.

I wish I could say that I sat down at a keyboard and in a moment, found "a computer virus with recursive encryption, very hard to crack" to the people who were not there to watch me. The truth is, in the end, the bad guys always win. Computer security is like a hockey game. The goalie can block a hundred shots on goal and still lose one to nothing.

It really didn't matter if Brandt was installing some kind of malware to, I would assume, give complete control of the machines to Lambeau. If they wanted to do that sort of thing, there was little I could do to stop them.

What concerned me is whether the malware would be well written. If it was quality bad guy stuff, I didn't care. If it was crappy bad guy stuff, it could hurt my machines and jeopardize the important work they do. If Frank had found his other rock star, he hadn't insulted me about it yet.

I talked the whole thing out with Ruth Ann later in bed. She agreed, with CB2 expected through here soon we had other things about which to worry. She also, as usual, had good advice. Also as usual, with me at least, she began bluntly.

"Back in California you know you acted like an ass. I can say that because I love you, right? You were a grade-A A-hole. Back there that was OK. I accepted that because that was your element."

I looked at her, paying attention, and keeping my mouth shut. Objecting when Ruth Ann was making "heartfelt observations" would only prolong the agony. I say agony not so much that it was annoying to hear her jabber on, no. It was annoying to hear the truth.

"When we moved back here, back to *my* element, you kept right on in your California mode. People were put off but you and I have thick skins. Neither of us really gives a poop what people think but after a while, it really started grating on me. Making friends in California was easy being married to an asshole because you were a powerful asshole. You were expected to be a jerk."

Being a jerk comes with the territory in the Valley. The bigger a prima donna you were the bigger your paycheck. Perceived value and all that. Nice people can't possibly know what they're doing.

"Besides, our friends weren't real friends. They were assholes on the rise. Sucking up to us to get ahead themselves. That one guy, you know the guy with the cheese name… Mario Ricotta, he was an aspiring ass. I bet he went home to that bleached blonde bimbo of his and said, 'You know honey, I want to be as big an asshole as Doug Handsman someday. Then people will really respect me.'"

"You made your point. I know you have another one."

"I'm getting to it. Every day lately, I am more and more amazed that it took the end of the world for you to become more human. You been showing empathy and compassion, attributes that could have gotten you fired in the Valley. You were excited about helping parents find their children. Where's the money in that?"

"My point is, Doug, you are growing as a person with everybody except Frank and Lambeau Field. You are still in A-hole, game playing, conniving, scheming, screw you mode. Just stop it all ready. Give it a rest."

"But hon, if I give him everything he wants there's less reason to rescue us."

"Doug, you caught Brandt fiddling with your rigs. You said yourself you can assume he already compromised your systems. If that is true, Lambeau is going to get what they want whether you give it to them or not. The smart thing to do is volunteer what they want. Give them everything before they have to ask again. Consider this a test."

"So this is a game and your observation is that I'm not playing it with the right strategy? Who is the scheming one again?"

"You know what I mean."

I hate that on so many levels. I hate it when the women in your life say that with an intensity that says they really think men *do* know what they mean. With that said, I knew what she meant.

◆ Wednesday (Day 42), was a good news / bad news kind of day.

I got up early and prepared all the code and scripts I've written and sent them off to Lambeau. In addition, I backed up the virtual servers and with them the databases that had been growing steadily. I sent all that off to Lambeau, a very large upload under any circumstances but made easier by an otherwise empty Gigabit connection. They now had a duplicate of the environment that existed here early this morning.

I did all this before talking to Frank in our late morning meeting. This way I could claim those altruistic team-player bennies Ruth Ann didn't quite say I should go for. This proved to be the right course of action as Frank's demeanor changed dramatically.

The really good news was that Milwaukee A was eviscerated by the B-52 strike the night before. Only an estimated hundred thousand creatures remained. Pretty soon they wouldn't be able to call it a horde.

More good news about MA, the remaining ghouls had been deflected slightly west. This meant they would run into the Fox River sooner. By the time MA reached the Green Bay area, it would undoubtedly be smaller due to the TO's that had already begun. Coming from the southwest rather than due south, what is left of MA may not even notice the Lambeau safe zone at all.

The overarching bad news was that while Lambeau was considerably safer, they would not be resuming TO's on Chicago B 2 until after they were sure they faced no significant threat. A B-52 strike like the one that was so successfully applied against MA would not be used in our defense. It was deemed that there was no "compelling strategic interest in expending the resources necessary for that kind of strike at this time."

There was no avoiding it. CB2 would be here for lunch around noon tomorrow.

As I helplessly watched CB2's inexorable march towards us on the satellite feed, I noticed something peculiar near Eau Claire. CB2 would trample the nearly demolished city that had already been the site of thinning operations and the eastward march of the Twin Cities horde. The horde would be through there early the next morning, a few hours before they hit Christmas Tree.

I was watching a lower-resolution stream. In the mostly brown and white landscape, some bright yellow dots stood out.

Ruth Ann was next to me at the kitchen table, practicing field stripping and cleaning a suppressed automatic rifle given to her by Bill Mancheski in recognition of her contribution to the home supply warehouse raid. She was as proud of her new acquisition as I was proud of her.

"Hey, look at this." I switched to the full resolution of the satellite stream. I centered on Carson Park in Eau Claire.

"Wow, that's a front loader and a bull dozer," Ruth Ann said.

Sure enough, in the magnified view we could see two pieces of heavy construction equipment tearing up Carson Park Drive, the only road leading into the park. The park itself sits at the end of a little peninsula jutting into Horseshoe Lake.

Little bits of the road disappeared with each fifteen-second update of the area.

"Look there. They are piling all the rubble and earth up there to make a berm behind the torn up road." Ruth Ann poked at the monitor with the pipe cleaner thing she was using to clear her weapon. It left a mark on the screen.

"I saw some infrared dots coming from there after we first got set up with the satellite but I thought it was small fires left over from the TO." If I had known to look more closely, I would have seen the fires burned in the same spot night to night, likely signs of survivors. I made a note to tell Frank that I could include specifically looking for campfires to the thinning operation optimization process without additional computational cost.

Spotting the earthmovers is how we learned of the encampment at Carson Park that I described earlier.

The survivors found construction equipment and were cutting themselves off more completely from the direction of CB2's progress. The daily radio updates kept everyone listening, including them, current on the horde's position and direction of march. While the survivors could not succeed in making an island out of the peninsula, cutting the easy access of the road left only dense woods leading into the heart of the park.

In cold weather, the dead typically follow a path of least resistance. With Carson Park Drive blocked by a high berm, the path of least resistance now led past the park. Stealth would keep them hidden.

The earthmovers moved off late in the morning. We could see where the yellow vehicles stopped through the partially denuded trees from our bird's eye view. The vehicles were driven back into the park quite a way so they would not be visible from the "mainland."

"We're not the only ones getting ready for CB2," Ruth Ann said.

"Speaking of getting ready, I'm off to find Bill and see what he's got the troops doing."

I toddled off leaving Ruth Ann to make sweet love to her rifle.

◆ I found Lieutenant Mancheski at the back of the house by the fuel cell generator. He, and several of his men, were looking into whatever could be done to silence what we thought was attracting the dead in a near continual dribble of ones and twos. The snipers on the roof kept walkers from encroaching upon the enclosed area surrounding the generator.

The bodies already spread around the fence were not uniformly distributed. Most lay nearest the spot where the natural gas used as a catalyst fed into the fuel cell itself. There was a distinct high-pitched hissing sound there. Bill had sent a pair of men out into the backyard to see how far the sound carried. Both reported they could no longer hear the sound a mere ten yards away.

Yet, the troops sent out on the home supply warehouse raid reported zombies walking with purpose in the direction of Christmas Tree from half a mile away.

Barry Clark, one of the men from the raid said "It has to be the hissing LT."

"That's the best lead we have. Hell, the hissing is the only lead we have. Lambeau has been no help at all," Mancheski said.

"When theaters in the home were first getting big…" I began.

"You mean home theaters?" interrupted Barry.

"*You* might mean home theater; *I* mean theaters in the home. This was California, after all. Anyway, an important step was sound absorbing blankets in the walls, floor and ceiling. They are dense felt blankets that are used like insulation only for sound," I said.

"And…" said Bill.

"I don't have any sound absorbing blankets on hand, but I do have insulation. You can send one of your men into the attic crawl space and bring some down. We might lose a little heat this winter, but it won't matter if we're dead."

"Barry, take Evans and pull down enough batting to wrap this whole section."

"Yes sir."

"I'll show you where the attic access is." I showed the two soldiers up to the second floor where, in a hallway ceiling there was an access panel leading to the crawl space above.

Soon the men had pulled down about eighty linear feet of insulation, enough to wrap several times over the area of pipes and tubes we believed was the corpse magnet.

Before the men applied the insulation I wanted to give the area one more sniff for leaking natural gas. I nosed around the area and smelled nothing but Barry Clark's body odor. That says a lot considering there were rotting zombies only a few feet away, but then again, they were well chilled.

Barry, on the other hand, had reached his "full flavor bouquet."

We had not had much snow since the day after the Twin Cities horde walked through Christmas Tree. The clouds filling in overhead suggested we'd get more snow soon. In fact, while I stood there watching the men wrap the insulation around the pipes, a few flakes began to fall.

It occurred to me that between the insulation now surrounding the natural gas pipes and the snow that was surely going to accumulate on the batting, if there was a gas leak there, it would make a nicely contained volume of gas. Enough to make a big boom. I dismissed this however as I had a sensitive nose and neither myself nor any of the men smelled gas when we poked around this area smelling for leaks.

◆ At eleven, Bill and I had our meeting with Frank.

"Thanks for getting all those backups to us Walter. Your people here tell me you were very thorough."

"They found the build and deployment instructions I wrote?" I was as solicitous as could be without reaching through the radio and nibbling on Frank's ears.

"I don't know what that means, but your people seemed happy. You'll be glad to know more resources are coming back online to help out in the event Christmas Tree needs evacuation."

"But the plan is till to hold tight, keep the datacenter running and hope CB2 passes us by?"

"Correct, that is still the plan. The battalion of self-propelled guns Lt. Mancheski requested has moved into position eleven miles south of you. They will be in touch with you later today to dial in their guns. Lieutenant, expect to hear from White Mountain Six, understood?"

"Heard and understood sir."

"Frank, this morning Mrs. Christmas Tree and I saw earth movers operating in Carson Park in Eau Claire. Do you know about an encampment there?"

"Hold Walter," Frank was probably bringing up maps.

"Carson Park, you say? No Walter, we have no knowledge of an encampment there. I wonder how they survived the thinning operations over Eau Claire."

"Do you have a current high resolution shot of the area in front of you?"

"I do now."

"OK. Look at Carson Park Drive as it starts into the park. You should see it being interrupted by an earthen embankment and the road in is cut. See that?"

"Yes I do. Pretty smart. The horde could pass them by. We figure CB2 will be on their position around 6 AM."

"That's what I estimate as well. Now look north northeast about five hundred yards. In the trees. You see the earth movers?"

"Got them Christmas Tree. If we bomb there again we will try to avoid Carson Park. Looks like we already demolished the little causeway leading to the park from the eastern side."

"I was thinking maybe you could swing by them sometime and drop supplies. Or maybe even pick them up when you get a chance."

"That's very thoughtful of you."

"Something else I was thinking about."

"Yes…"

"We shouldn't have missed spotting them in the first place. The optimizers take in multiple high-resolution captures to measure size, speed and direction of the hordes. It would not be hard to extend my part of the code to look for infrared signatures indicating small fires at night. I'm sure we could find a lot of survivors that way. I'd like to add that feature after CB2 passes by or we're evacuated."

Nudge, nudge.

I continued, "So it is OK with you if I just keep existing things running until after CB2 passes? I can keep up with my people by email to keep them making progress but for me I don't think I can wrap my head around new coding right now."

"It's a good idea Walter. One more time you are ahead of the curve for us. Finding isolated survivors will rise in priority as the security of the established safe zones becomes more certain."

"Speaking of that, how are things looking for you in Door County?"

"Good. Things are looking good. We have a solid defensive line set up including all the mobile pill boxes the command authority can spare. Demolition charges are strategically placed throughout Green Bay and the bridges across the Fox River to help direct the horde's flow if it notices us. We're still hopeful they will flow past us to the west and through Green Bay proper."

"I hope all the entrances to the real Lambeau are shut tight."

"They are. We sent teams in there to ensure that facility was secured. Once this is over Packer football will return to Green Bay. The rumors are that the Bears will share Lambeau while Chicago is decontaminated. Reconnaissance flights over Chicago still show considerable activity in the city. Even inside Soldier Field."

"Bears being the home team in Lambeau? I would rather share the stadium with zombies."

"Walter…"

"Yes Frank."

"I'm from Chicago."

"My condolences to you."

◆ Over lunch, we listened to the public broadcast from Lambeau. Steady progress had been made in Puerto Rico since I last wrote about the world beyond Christmas Tree. As I said at the outset of this book, other authors can provide more details about the larger world than I.

What makes today special is that the first session of the reconstituted United States Senate was held in the nation's new Capitol. The House of Representatives couldn't meet because no one can agree on how many representatives should be allotted to each state. Ruth Ann's Mendocino Mind Fuck fueled prediction of a demographic and population change taking place, because of the apocalypse, was coming true.

Even as Conservatives appeared to be cementing power, one of the cornerstones of their delusion, religion, was taking a beating. A newly minted Senator from Texas wanted a statement of thanks to God for preserving the Union read into the record. He was shouted down and, borrowing from a lesson on decorum from the South Korean National Assembly, was pelted with (full) water bottles and trash.

Apparently, people were waking up to the idea that God couldn't be thanked without taking the blame for the horrific events of the past six weeks. God's get-out-jail-free card had been suspended at least for a while.

My own thought was, why should we believe reconstituting the Senate was something worth being thankful for in the first place?

The news segment closed with the announcement that hearings into the Benghazi embassy attack would resume.

Changing the members of the Senate, changing the location of the Senate, killing hundreds of millions of constituents of the Senate could not change the ideology of the Senate. Back to square gridlock.

◆ At one in the afternoon Bill Mancheski invited Ruth Ann and I up to our roof to observe "something really cool." When we arrived, Bill was talking into his personal radio. Bill handed Ruth Ann and I each a Kevlar helmet borrowed from the men who were off duty.

He said, "Just in case."

"In case of what?" I asked.

As the words left my lips an enormous burst of colored smoke appeared near where the Xian's house had stood.

"White Mountain Six, this is Christmas Tree Six. Correction twenty meters east, ten meters south."

I thought I heard something sharp coming through the softly falling snow.

Another giant ball of colored smoke appeared directly over the wreckage of Xian's house.

"White Mountain Six, this is Christmas Tree Six. Mark last shot two houses north one block east of Christmas Tree." Bill said to the other end of the conversation.

He listened then motioned for us to move to the eastern facing parapet wall and get down lower.

In a moment I heard the sound I heard before only more clearly. Sort of like a quickly repeated crack of a baseball bat.

An enormous burst of colored smoke burst over the wreckage of Olson's house directly east of us.

"White Mountain Six, you are dialed in," Bill said. Then he listened for a moment then nodded his head.

"We hope we don't need you too. Christmas Tree Six out."

Bill turned to us and said, "Cool huh? They're eleven miles away."

"How can they be so accurate over the distance? How do they account for wind variations?" asked Ruth Ann.

"They use a variant of PFM," Bill said in reply.

"PFM?"

"Pure Magic. I am completely satisfied knowing they *can* be that accurate. I don't really care *how*."

"What is the variation?" I stupidly said.

"The missing letter F," said Bill.

I should have seen that coming.

"How is artillery going to be useful to us?" said Ruth Ann.

"I don't know. It may help to burn what's left of your neighbor's houses."

With the exception of the Boetch's house to our west, all of the homes nearby were breached, either by looters, or by the undead or by looters and the undead. Any home that showed a sign of having been breached had been demolished by Bill's squad or the other team that arrived one week before.

"Or, maybe shrouding us in smoke might help. I won't know until I know," Bill finished.

"I wish Frank would be forthcoming with details about the resources he has available for us should things go south here," Ruth Ann said.

"He mentioned assets from the North Western Administrative Zone would be shifted our way. Do you know thing more about that Bill?"

I said this with a sideways glance at Bill Mancheski. Apart from a willingness to put a gun to my head and pull the trigger if ordered to do so, Bill hadn't given me any reason to believe he wasn't playing straight with us. Then again, Brandt hadn't given me any cause to doubt him either.

"I heard Lambeau welcome two flights of gunships from North Dakota into their command and control net."

"Do you know where they went?"

"Yes, they are using Brainerd Lakes Regional Airport as a base of operations."

"Where is that exactly?"

I felt like I was talking to Ryan Boetch again. If Bill used the word "fine," I swear I would have put a gun to his head and pulled the trigger. No offense to Bill intended.

Bill shrugged and said "Minnesota."

I made a beeline to my laptop. On it, I had a travel-planning package with good maps. All I needed was the latitude and longitude of the airport and I would be able to figure out how far away they are. Maybe I'd even get a look at their hardware from a satellite view.

Go figure, I found Brainerd Lakes Regional Airport near Brainerd, in central Minnesota. The small airport was a little over 150 miles from Christmas Tree.

I pulled up a current high-resolution satellite image of the area and saw no military hardware of any kind. There was a helipad and hangars but nothing else. The only thing suggestive of any presence by anyone was that all of the aviation fuel trucks I could see were gathered near the larger hangars at the main runway. There was more than enough room in front of the building to launch and land many helicopters.

"I hope there is somebody in there," Ruth Ann said over my shoulder.

"Me too. They are close enough. That's good."

◆ Preparations inside the house were relatively little. To sum up, there was nothing we could do to shore up defenses inside Christmas Tree.

If we lost the second floor, there was no way to hold the first floor with just open plan staircases between them. Knowing this to be true did not make me feel any better as I watched explosive charges being wired to the stairs.

Ruth Ann directed two soldiers in stockpiling supplies in the basement. There were already stores of emergency food and canned goods down there, though the home canned delicacies such as strawberry jam were all but gone.

As electricity might fail and with it the water pump after my own batteries gave out, anything that could contain water was brought down stairs and filled.

I took Brandt into the machine room for “last instructions.” Brandt was to be stationed in the basement along with Ruth Ann and I to defend us or the machines, I don’t know which.

“I backed everything up to Lambeau this morning so this shouldn’t be important. But, just in case, the one thing in this room you should care about taking out of here is this box right here.”

I pointed to one of the two Networked Attached Storage boxes, about the size of a four small loaves of bread stacked two by two.

“This box has a complete copy of the backup I sent this morning. It is off, disconnected and ready to go. This box. Not that one. OK?”

“Got it. This one, not that one.” Brandt took out a small roll of tape from one of the hundreds of little pockets the soldiers seemed to have. He stuck a strip of tape on the correct box making it visibly different from its twin.

“I showed you this when you got here but it wouldn’t hurt to show you again. This is the switch from the mains to battery power. If, …”

"We lose the generator, throw that switch if it doesn't switch automatically," Brandt interrupted.

"The machines will cut out when, sorry, if the generator cuts out. The Internet will still be live, as will the cameras. They run off the batteries. If we lose the solar panels and the generator, we have to use hand-cranked devices as much as possible. At minimal consumption, we have enough batteries to last a week. Then we are blind and dry with hand cranked devices only."

At least we would have lights and a radio. Brandt had finished bringing the tactical radio into the basement and rigging a means of getting the external antenna outside the house. I did not ask nor did I want to know how he breached my precious concrete walls.

Ruth Ann had gone up to the roof with Bill.

"Do you believe for a minute that the horde won't pile up enough bodies to reach the roof?" said Ruth Ann.

"No. You are right Mrs. Handsman. The fuel cell is just a step from the side of the house. If they pile on top of each other enough to get over the fence, they will definitely get onto the top of the generator then hoist themselves onto the roof."

"Yet you won't board up the roof door. There are no physical barriers between the roof door all the way downstairs to the basement door."

"My orders are to keep the datacenter running as long as possible. To do that I need men on the roof keeping Zeke off the generator. The men have to have a way down. We can rig the stairways to blow."

"That works when zombies are below you Bill, not for zombies above you. Doug and I saw zombies fall out of the Flynn's deck door to the ground and get right back up. They'll drop right through like lemmings over a cliff, only they won't die when the hit the bottom."

"Those are my orders. Keep the datacenter running."

“At least take the second hasp from the front door and put it up here on the roof.”

“I’ll do that. The front door isn’t going to budge.”

Bill made it so.

We spent the rest of the day in nervous boredom. I watched the horde advance. The soldiers cleaned and checked their weapons. I asked Barry Clark to take a long shower.

◆ The day had finally come. Thursday (Day 43), we all rose early and had a substantial breakfast of dried eggs and cereal with powdered milk. We simulated toast with saltine crackers and used home canned pumpkin butter.

A heavy snow had continued during the night covering everything. Winds had caused drifts of snow up against the fence enclosing the fuel cell system.

Several dead, who had escaped the terminal welcome offered by our snipers during the night, had already climbed the fence. We found them at first light slowly grabbing into the space between the natural gas tanks and the generator itself. The Specialist on camera duty had not seen them breach our defense due to the snow.

Bob and Bob took careful aim and turned the zombie's lights out, dropping them directly onto the device keeping our lights on.

Bill sent men out to shovel away the drifts at the base of the fence. The drifts made it easier to climb the fence. The snow had stopped, but the wind hadn't. Drifts returned soon thereafter. Keeping them away from the fence would be a lost cause.

At six twenty, the starkly visible horde of dark on white trampled past Carson Park. We watched tensely on the big screen as it enveloped and crushed what was left of Eau Claire. So far, we saw no activity inside the park so all seemed well for the survivors inside. They would be surrounded for hours to come.

CB2 was now only a few hours away from us.

At six thirty, we saw a flight of helicopters destroy what was left of the eastern causeway between the mainland and the peninsula of the park itself. They left the Carson Park Drive area alone, apparently satisfied with what the survivors had done for themselves.

We topped off the water containers we had been using. Bob Wisnewski swept off the solar panels. The men checked ammunition and weapons.

Bill and I had an early meeting with Frank.

"You can see the drifting snow has made it easier to scale the fence around the generator. The damn thing is attracting the dead like gun shots," I said.

"Sir, I request permission to disengage the fuel cell generator," added Bill.

"The request is denied Christmas Tree. The datacenter must remain running for as long as possible. We have serious situations in a number of Administrative Zones that need the results you produce. The hordes are getting hungrier. They are more aggressive if you can imagine that. A number of safe zones are in peril as we speak. Do you understand your orders Lieutenant?"

"Yes sir. Hua."

◆ I gave up trying to have the generator switched off. In my resignation, I changed subjects.

"Frank, we may not make it through this. There's one thing I want to know," I said.

"Walter, there's no reason to get maudlin. We will keep you safe."

"No really. We've had this Father Goose Frank and Walter code name business going since the beginning. I have to know. What is your real name?"

"Frank."

"Frank?"

"Frank."

"Your code name is your real name. Seriously?"

"I never said it was a code name. You were to be Christmas Tree. I told you my name, you came up with 'Walter,' I just went with it."

Off mike, I said to Bill, "You knew about this?"

"Of course. I had no idea why he called you Walter and Ruth Ann Miss Goody Two Shoes. Is Father Goose a movie?" Bill said.

Back on mike I said "Attention all listening stations this is Doug and Ruth Ann Handsman signing off from Christmas Tree. Good night and good luck."

"That was touching Walter. Sit tight. We'll talk again. Lambeau Field out."

◆ Bill and I looked at each other and took a deep breath in. Then he shouted, "Gather up people!"

Bill was joined by his ten men.

"CB2 will be here soon. There are millions of them and the god damned fuel cell thing is going to bring them here like flies on a honey wagon. Our orders are to keep the datacenter running as long as possible. Doing so will save lives," Bill paused and looked into his troop's faces.

"To do that, we have to keep the generator on."

Another pause.

"I want three volunteers to man the roof to keep the generator clear. I don't have to tell you, you will likely die."

"I'll go," Bob Peretz said.

"You stupid kike, what are you volunteering me for?" said Bob Wisnewski.

"I didn't volunteer you, you dumb Polack."

"Sure you did, you know I got your back. Where you go I go."

"I'm going on the roof," said Peretz.

"OK man. I got your back."

"That's two. I need one more."

Leon Cremmons, a quiet Specialist I hardly knew was the third volunteer to face a likely death on the roof of Christmas Tree.

"Thank you men. Take whatever you need and dig in up there. Sweep Zeke off the generator but try not to blow it up yourselves. Good luck."

The doomed three shook hands and said good byes to their brothers. Then they went off to gather gear and headed up stairs.

"Brandt, you're in the basement. Your job is to protect the gear and specifically that box Mr. Handsman told you about. Whatever you do, that box has to be kept safe, understand?"

No mention of protecting us.

"Hua," was Brandt's reply.

"Barry, Orderly, you're in the basement too. Your job is to keep Mr. and Mrs. Handsman safe. Hua?"

"Hua," both said.

There's that, I thought.

Brandt and Clark looked determined. Orderly look relieved.

"Lim, you me and John will stay on the second floor. It won't be a picnic, the windows are our weak spots. We can fall back to the first floor if need be."

Lim Zsu, who accompanied Mancheski into the warehouse and John Rentmiesters who also went on the raid would stick by their Lieutenant once again.

"Chuck and Chris, you are in reserve on one. The only way they are getting to the first floor is if the wheels come off the wagon. Your job is to hold the door to the basement and cover us on the way down, got it?"

"Hua," said Chris Sanders who I didn't know and Chuck Evans who had been in on the warehouse raid.

"OK, people. Let's do it."

The volunteers on the roof were locked out. From here on until their quickly approaching end, they were on their own.

Furniture from the first floor was moved to barriers against the second windows. Only the windows near the generator were covered on the outside with glued plywood. A heavy couch and chair were wedged into the stairway leading to the roof. There really wasn't a point to barricading the stairway between the first and second floors. Doing so wouldn't prevent us from being overrun but would hamper any retreat attempt by Bill, Lim and John.

Ruth Ann and I, along with Brandt, Orderly and Barry locked ourselves into the basement. I isolated the well, Internet router, modem and the house camera system to the battery backups. If we lost generator power, while the datacenter would crash instantly, we would still have water, surveillance and two ways of contacting Lambeau. The NAS box containing a complete backup of Christmas Tree was disconnected and ready for bug out.

We watched the satellite view of CB2 as it converged on Christmas Tree from both north and south. Whether drawn by the sound of the generator or just bad luck, CB2 came down on us like a closing pincer.

The remains of our neighbor's houses to the east and north imploded into their basements under thousands of highly agitated ghouls.

Giant fire balls erupted between Christmas Tree and its neighbors. The mobile artillery made its presence known. High explosives are loud but the sound of the exploding shells did not overpower the sound of the horde itself.

Bob and Bob along with Leon Cremmons opened up on the horde as it easily rose up and over the fence surrounding the fuel cell generator. It was immediately obvious leaving those men up there to die was a complete waste. Nothing would have stopped the generator from being overrun except the stealth provided by being turned off before the horde arrived.

On my laptop, we watched the dead tumble off the top of the generator fence. More and more made it into the tight space between the fence and the generator.

On the other cameras, we could see the dead coming closer and closer to camera level like rising floodwater. They climbed over each other rising towards roof level. Just before the southward facing cameras became blocked by constantly churning darkness we saw them spilling in through the windows on the second floor.

There would be no prolonged heroic siege. Christmas Tree did not stand firm against a raging ocean of dead. No, we were slammed hard under in the first unstoppable wave.

We heard automatic weapons fire both through the basement door and on the radio. Lim was already dead. John Rentmiesters body checked Bill, tossing him down stairway leading to the first floor.

Evans and Sanders pulled Bill to his feet. For a moment they stood, weapons pointing upward, while the John Rentmiesters assault rifle howled.

I looked down at the laptop screen and saw that bodies were still tumbling off the roof near the generator. The doomed men on the roof were still firing.

Then they were tumbling off the generator *itself.*

Barely had I breathed "No" the cameras to the rear of the house showed a blinding flash and went dead. The house shook so violently cracks appeared in the basement ceiling. The datacenter went instantly silent.

For a moment, the surviving cameras were clear of writhing bodies. The explosion the generator was so great that zombies were temporarily shaken from their purchase. The two remaining cameras facing westward showed a massive fire. The northwest facing view showed flames billowing out of the second floor windows.

In the few seconds lull afforded by the explosion, Sanders banged on the basement door. Over the radio he said, "Open dammit. We're coming in."

Brandt and Clark were at the ready at the top landing. Brandt shouted "Clear!" and push open the door. Bill Mancheski and Chris Sanders tumbled inside at knee level. Over them, Brandt fired his weapon but as he did so, putrid arms grabbed him. They lifted him off his feet, over Mancheski and Sanders. In an instant, Brandt was gone. In the feeding frenzy that erupted, Barry Clark was able to slam the solid door shut and locked it.

Willem. Brandt's first name was Willem.

Mancheski and Clark carried Sanders down stairs where we could see, by the light of crank driven lanterns, ragged claw marks through Sanders tattered uniform. Sanders, his arms already swollen with bites, lay limply at the bottom of the stairs.

Bill Mancheski stripped quickly. We searched his body for broken skin. He was bruised and dirty with what might have been blood, but it was not his. The shield that was his thin layer of skin had held.

Chris Sanders barely breathed now. His skin was gray.

There was no drama as in the prewar movies and books. Bill, still naked, simply said, “Barry, can I have your sidearm?”

Barry handed his pistol to Bill.

Bill looked at all of us and looked at Chris. Then he fired once into Chris’s head.

Barry and Orderly rolled Chris Sanders’ body into a blanket and dragged it into the now silent machine room.

Bill Mancheski got dressed.

“What is our situation?” he said.

“Cameras at the back of the house are gone. So is the one at the northeast corner. The other cameras are blocked by Zombies. Sometimes daylight pokes through. There are a lot of flames,” I said flatly.

There was no point in asking about Evans.

The banging and clawing at the basement door was intense.

Thinking what we were all thinking, Bill said, “The basement door will hold. The fire will take out the landing’s walls before that door breaks. Does the radio work?”

“Negative,” said Orderly. “The explosion must have destroyed the antenna. We can’t get a signal down here.”

“But we still have an Internet connection,” I said. “Lambeau sees what the cameras see. We should have battery power for a few days.”

“Let’s drop them a line,” Bill said sounding like it was the most ordinary thing in the world.

“Tell them eight KIA and five survivors in the basement. Radio is down. We have food, water and battery reserves. Request immediate rescue.”

I typed and sent the email.

We waited.

Back in the earliest days of email, one girlfriend or another dumped me. I was depressed. I sat at the UNIX shell prompt reentering "mail" repeatedly only to see "no mail" appear each time. I felt like that now. I get clicking on the email refresh button willing a reply to come.

In what seemed like hours but was no more than a few minutes, we got our two-word reply.

"Sit tight."

After I read this aloud, over the din of the banging, kicking and scraping coming from the basement door Barry Clark expressed his dissatisfaction with the brevity of the answer.

"Sit tight? That's it? That is all they fucking said?"

"Barry, calm down. What else are we supposed to do? We're trapped down here. Whether we burn to death, die of thirst, starvation, kill each other, die from smoke inhalation, get crushed or get eaten, we're not going anywhere," said Orderly.

Sergeant Orderly looked like he could have continued ticking off ways we could die for another long while. Thankfully, he stopped where he did. Barry flung his arms out in a vigorous "what-the-hell?" motion and sat down. Tight.

The ceiling above us creaked and groaned under the weight of who knows how many zombies crashing about above us. The banging on the door was incessant.

For a moment, body parts cleared from camera four, replaced by fire. Then the feed went dark.

Moments later, there was a rumble like the sound of falling concrete, which in fact it was. Part of the back wall of the house had given way out of view of any of the remaining cameras.

We could smell the odor of burning house quite distinctly now. There is the pleasant smell of a neighbor's wood fire grill or a fireplace on a winter's night. There is the pleasant smell of a campfire. Then there is the smell of burning house. It is different. It is not pleasant.

Ruth Ann soaked some towels in water and with Orderly accompanying her to the top landing, placed them at the base of door. When she returned, she told us that the door did not feel warm. Yet.

The smell of smoke did not decrease. In the dim light of our lanterns we could see smoke, dust and small bits of debris drop from the ceiling vents. The air in the basement has to be drawn from somewhere. The growing haze told us the source of what we were breathing.

Email!

This email was as terse as the last.

“Rescue arrives in thirty minutes. Say state.”

After a brief discussion, we sent back:

“Smoke inhalation likely to kill us before then. Hurry.”

There was an attachment to the email we received. I opened it up and saw that it was a reasonably close up aerial view of Christmas Tree. Above us somewhere, out of reach, somebody was looking over the carnage. The picture showed too many creatures to count. Flames emanated from the rear of the house and the northeast corner had indeed caved in.

There were dark gaps in the fire, which, when I zoomed in, were roasting zombies. Everywhere there were zombies packed more tightly than any living human could tolerate.

“Rescue? How can they get us out of a burning building in the middle of a horde? How is that possible?” Ruth Ann said.

There was no need to speak in hushed tones in face of the din thundering from upstairs.

“Now that the fuel cell system isn’t drawing them to us anymore the crowd here at the house should go down,” I said hopefully.

Indeed, I could see daylight more often in the cameras that were still operational. The crush of bodies climbing over themselves to get to us was thinning out.

The pounding on the basement door continued mercilessly as did the groaning of the ceiling above us. The dead howled and roared. We could hear the hum of the fire.

"We have to stop the smoke from coming down here," Barry said.

"But we can't seal up the vents completely, we need air," Bill added. "The vent over there is furthest from the fire. Do you have more cloth to cover the rest?"

"Yeah, Barry, help me get down some sheets and soak them in the sink," Ruth Ann rose.

While they did that, I told Bill about one more way we could die.

"You know the door area isn't their only way in. If the fire penetrates the first floor anywhere, we'll be a soft chewy snack."

"I know. Nothing we can do about it."

Barry and Ruth Ann returned with the white soaked sheets, hammer, and nails. They went to each of the vents closest to the fire and covered them.

Orderly stood watch at the bottom of the basement stairs.

We waited.

Ruth Ann kept the sheets covering the vents wet. They sagged and got darker by the minute.

It was getting hard to breath.

The cameras were clear of writhing bodies now, though covered with dirt, pus and who knows what else. We were still in the middle of a horde but its members were now slowly milling past us rather than over us.

The noise from the zombies inside the house lessened. Maybe the fire that would soon suffocate us or open a hole in the landing or first floor for the horde to pour in, was consuming them. We did not know.

I was feeling woozy.

◆ The sound at the stairway seemed to get louder. The three soldiers moved into position at the bottom of the stairs. The foundation started shaking. Through the cameras, I could see high explosives ring the house in a circle at the limits of the camera's sight.

Suddenly the men's radios came alive. Rescue was dropping out of the sky above us.

No sooner did the radios erupt, sheetrock that used to form one wall of the stairway broke apart and fell. The shards of sheetrock were on fire as were the zombies that dropped into the stairwell with them.

The soldiers opened up with everything they had.

I don't know if it was the cumulative stress, the deafening noise, oxygen deprivation or what, I felt myself slipping away. Rescue was now or…

◆ The right side of my face was pushed against a wall. Somebody was yelling at me to do something. I could not tell what it was.

My hearing wasn't working right.

The fog lifted enough for me to realize we were in the short vestibule leading to the inner garage door on the right and the laundry room on the left. Despite my confusion, I saw the inner garage door was missing. If light was coming through the door, I thought, the door should be swung open into the house. It wasn't there. That was strange.

There was a helmet blocking the light. It connected to a moving body. Shit. Zombies wearing military issue helmets were hard to put down. Ah, good. The figure isn't trying to eat anyone. It must be a living person.

The figure was looking through the door. He was holding something down and against the wall, in the same way as I was being held. It was Ruth Ann. My wife.

Like being shocked awake by cold water, the cobwebs rapidly cleared.

The door was blasted off its hinges, the doorframe mangled.

The soldier holding Ruth Ann suddenly turned to her. He tried to take the assault rifle Ruth Ann held.

She resisted.

"We have to go *now!* We'll get you another one!"

Ruth Ann let go. The soldier laid it at the feet of another soldier firing bursts towards the laundry room window.

Together, Ruth Ann and the soldier shielding her disappeared through the door.

My protector shoved me forward. Then it was our turn to run.

He grabbed me by my shoulder with such force I almost lost my grip on the Network Attached Storage box under my right arm. That was when I realized I was holding it. Brandt was supposed to be carrying the box. He was dead.

Our Volvo wagon was just outside the house. Its windows were broken but otherwise looked ready for a Sunday drive. I have no idea how they moved it out of the garage.

Small fires burned in the garage but we were safe to pass through.

As we rushed out to a large twin rotor helicopter, my range of vision expanded. I saw on either side of the garage Special Forces firing on full automatic away from the house. As I said before, firing on full automatic means you are in deep shit. Zombie parts lay everywhere.

These men were the innermost of layers of destruction carving a minute or two of space for our evacuation.

Now outside the garage, I could see gunships hovering above us. Streaks of leaden light from their Gatling guns cut a mote separating Christmas Tree from the CB2 horde.

To the south, a surprisingly small distance beyond the curtain of gunships, a line of high explosives rained down. These were courtesy of the self-propelled howitzers eleven miles away. Damn, they were accurate.

We ran to the waiting rear door of the cargo helicopter. Gatling gun and heavy machine gun fire streamed from both sides of the chopper.

The noise inside the garage was incredible. It was nothing compared to the sound that assaulted me when we broke the confines of my burning home.

One Gatling gun sounds like a table saw. A dozen sounds like a whole sawmill. Below them in pitch, sounding even more deadly was the constant staccato of heavy machine guns. Howitzers played timpani drums. Helicopter rotors and the howling of tens of thousands of ghouls made up a call and continuous answer of a massive chorus.

Men dragged me roughly up the lowered cargo door. Bill Mancheski, Orderly and Barry Clark were right behind us. The Special Forces members collapsed their circle of covering fire quickly backing up to the cargo door. The door started to close as the helicopter began to rise.

◆ The last time I saw Christmas Tree, flames shot through the roof where our garden and solar panels had been. Crawling like enraged soldier ants, thousands of zombies made a mound over the burning roof. Still more were coming up over the backs of others, trying to get at the humans who had been there only a moment before.

Beyond them, my yard boiled with merging arms and bodies, too thick to identify as individuals. As we ascended, the boiling froth went on and on until it looked like storm tossed waves from the air.

Ruth Ann and I held hands.

Though we could not see the flames any more, the pillar of smoke that rose from our home was visible for a long time.

After a while, it too was gone.

◆ It has been eighteen months since the events in this book occurred. Of the eleven troops stationed at Camp Christmas Tree, three survived. Ruth Ann and I, along with Bill Mancheski, Orderly and Barry Clark were airlifted to Brainerd Minnesota where we rested overnight. From there, we flew to Door County.

Each of the soldiers went through their own debriefing process, given some rest, then were sent off to new assignments.

Barry went to what now passed for Officers Training School and is now on the front line in California as a Lieutenant.

Bill Mancheski is now Captain Mancheski. He landed in the first wave on Long Island, Orderly right by his side.

Orderly died recently. There was not a scratch on him. Being summer, the virus is airborne again. We liked Sergeant Orderly very much.

Ruth Ann and I finally met Frank. Colonel Franklin Schebielski turned out to be a short powerfully built cigar-smoking career Army Intelligence officer. He liaises with a classified number of small groups of survivors getting what utility he can out of them while helping them cope with their circumstances. We keep in touch from time to time.

Ryan Boetche works as a technical expert for The Internal Revenue Service tracking down illegal grow operations. Marijuana is still legal, just taxed.

The web site bringing parents and children together born at Christmas Tree was spun out as a non-profit operating in over 100 countries. Ruth Ann is its director.

As for me, I cannot tell you what I do. It's classified.

The main character of this story remains a burned out shell. Only some of the concrete first floor walls still stand. Though the chance of another horde in the area is remote, it isn't safe enough yet for repopulation. There are a number of computer-controlled rifles in the area. They are newer, more expensive descendants of the one I pitched to Lambeau to defend shorelines.

They still go off a lot.

www.ingramcontent.com/pod-product-compliance
Lightning Source LLC
Chambersburg PA
CBHW071310200626
46813CB00015B/954
* 9 7 8 0 9 8 9 2 1 2 8 1 6 *